T0096826

The Scrapbook

The Scrapbook

Carly Holmes

Parthian
The Old Surgery
Napier Street
Cardigan
SA43 1ED
www.parthianbooks.com

First published in 2014
© Carly Holmes 2014
All Rights Reserved

ISBN 978-1-909844-57-5

Editor: Susie Wild
Cover design by www.theundercard.co.uk
Front cover image © Cathy Stocker 2013/www.cathystocker.com
Printed and bound by Gomer Press, Llandysul, Wales

Published with the financial support of the Welsh Books
Council

British Library Cataloguing in Publication Data

A cataloguing record for this book is available from the British
Library.

For my lost ones: Luna, Goblin, Moomin

Variation On A Love Spell

Take in your cupped palms
two flaming pieces of fire opal
and two gentling pieces of rose quartz.
Linger a while with sweet thoughts.

Lash each crystal to your chest with a plait of red silk
lined above your heart's beat
and leave them for five days and nights.
Never allow so much as a sliver of breath to separate
them from the warmth and touch of your flesh.

Glaze these crystals with your body's sweat.
Paint loving pictures in your mind's eye.
Rise to meet each morning with harmony
and greet your pillow each night with desire.

On the sixth day remove one of each crystal but leave its
twin on your skin. While they are still warm from your
heart, still wet from your ardour
gift the removed crystals to your lover.
They must be kept as close to your lover's skin as possible.

If this spell is surreptitiously cast then use your wiles to
secrete the crystals
where their magics can be felt but not found.
After three days and nights the fire you lit in another's
soul will spark
and you will know the heat of true devotion.

The stronger your longings,
The stronger the charge,
The stronger the love.

Take care to never lose the crystals after they have secured your desire.
Keep all four safely wrapped up together where no harm can come to them.

If you wish for your shared love to transcend mortality then ensure that you are both buried with your crystals.
It matters little by this stage whose were originally whose.

Be sure and be true to your love for evermore.
A certain manipulation of their original fate will be your cross to bear.

I

I was four the first time I attacked my father. My memory of it is sulking behind twenty-odd years of bicycle tumbles and birthday parties, first kisses and fierce heartbreaks, and so I only have my mum's account to rely on. Depending on her mood, and how much she's had to drink, I'm either painted as a strange, difficult child (buoyant, first gin), or an out and out child of Satan, practically gnashing my teeth and straining towards people's throats (weepy, finishing that one too many).

Such an angry little girl... So embarrassing... I couldn't take you anywhere...

The fragments I do recall are the smell of sun-scorched leaves and the back of my mum's head. She stood by the window in the front room and shivered from foot to foot, releasing layers of fruity scent with each warm tremble of excitement. Even now, if I dip my face into a bowl of peaches I feel bereft, just for a second.

I knelt behind her and itched to touch my clammy fingers to the filmy hem of her dress. It must have been summertime.

Granny Ivy sat hunched like a raven in a rainstorm and stabbed thick thread violently through one of my dresses, sewing a pocket onto it. She muttered constantly to herself, occasionally pausing to peer at me or to press a thin finger against the dark, cracked book she always kept by her side until the day it disappeared. Her *Cooking Book*, she called it, which always made mum snort.

The only ingredients you've got in there are toad's eyeballs and hen's claws.

So, mum stood, and shivered, and glanced over her shoulder but didn't shift from her vigil.

Fern, stop staring at me... Fern, get up off the floor...

And then she was gone. I blinked and looked away, as instructed, and movement tangled suddenly in the corner of my eye. The front door was wide open and I could still smell her, but she'd disappeared. I leaned over and looked for the puff of smoke, straining after her absence even as she returned, smiling and joyful.

Lawrence is here. I'm off now.

She stood in the centre of the room as if she'd never left it and tapped her feet and crossed her arms. I shuffled backwards, away from those mean looking high heels.

Don't wait up.

Granny Ivy hissed and jerked and the needle slipped deep into her palm. She and mum stared at each other and I watched the blood drip over the brand new pocket of my dress. I'd chosen the pocket myself from old curtain material and I wanted to point at the rusty stain as it ruined the beautiful pink cabbage roses, wanted to shout something at them both to break their concentration. But then a man walked into the room and straight up to me. I hadn't heard a knock at the door.

Hello, Fern.

Mum snapped out of her hard face and into her soft one. She took the man's arm and hugged it to her.

Fern, say hello.

I looked at this man being held by my mother. I glanced over at Granny Ivy, then back.

Who are you?

There was silence. Then Granny Ivy sniggered and shot me a look that meant there'd be biscuits before bedtime. Mum laughed brightly, for too long. She bent down and showed me her hard face again, just for a second, just for me.

He's your father. Now stop being silly and say hello.

She straightened up and laughed again, turned to the man with a shrug of hopeless mirth. He grimaced at her and crouched down next to me, legs creaking inside soft grey cloth. I imagined wooden knee joints and wondered if he was a puppet. A huge hand descended onto my head, pressed my hairgrips into my scalp and hurt me. I wriggled and tried to duck away but couldn't slip out from under his palm.

Hello, Fern.

Mum scooped up her handbag and glanced at her watch.

Say hello to your father, Fern... Fern, say hello...

I dived forward to escape them both and then flung myself onto his chest. Thrust upwards as high and as hard as I could, as if I was a swimmer and he was the water. I grabbed a handful of his hair in each fist. And I pulled.

It took them ages to uncurl my hands and drag me off him. By the time they'd managed it the man was scarlet and breathing noisily through his mouth and my mother was white and stiff. I scuttled to hide under Granny Ivy's long skirt, clutching strands of oily, mousy coloured hair. The man smoothed the front of his jacket, tried to smile, and turned away.

I'll be in the car, Iris.

He hadn't looked at Granny Ivy once in the whole time he'd been inside her home, and she hadn't looked at him.

My mother rushed to follow, pausing to point a finger at the bulge I made under my granny's chair. She mouthed speechless outrage and jabbed the air with menace.

After they'd gone – and this I remember very clearly – Granny Ivy gently removed all of the strands of the man's hair from my hands, untwisted them from my fingers and inspected my palms for any stragglers. Then she tucked the greasy bundle inside the cover of her *Cooking Book* and patted my back.

Good girl… Don't cry…

I followed the midnight billow of her skirts through to the kitchen and wondered if she was going to leave the hairs out on the sill for the birds to take away for their nests. I watched her to see if she would but then she placed a tin of biscuits down in front of me – the whole tin – and I was distracted for a while. We sat at the table and I crunched through bitter chocolate and fierce ginger while she watched me and smiled. She brewed tea and then opened her book, flickering through the pages as I reached for another biscuit, and then another. I wondered what she'd be making for supper.

Granny Ivy caught my wrist as it dived once more into the tin. She ran a nail along the knobbled warts that bumped a line down my middle finger. I sat with a biscuit in each fist and another in my cheek and listened as she began to speak.

*Search and you will find
a large, smooth sprout
hanging low upon the stalk,
defying the helix,
and paler than its mates.*

*This is the one.
Sharpen your knife
and slice.
Two halves. Two wrinkled hearts.*

Press firm and hard this wrinkled heart of one half onto
the wart.
Press, and count the minutes down from five to one.
Rejoin the halves and bind with string
and bury beside an oak tree.

The sprout now an oyster beneath the earth
cradling your wart in its rotting heart.

Remember not to ever dig around this buried vessel
or expose it to sunlight
or skin
as the wart will sense its kin
and cleave with you once more.

She continued to mutter as she stood up and fetched her sharp, wooden-handled knife from the cutlery drawer. I sneaked another biscuit and went to the window to watch as she prowled around the vegetable patch, bending, straightening, shaking her head and bending again.

It was only later, years later, I realised that her *Cooking Book* wasn't a recipe book in the strictest sense. At the time, as I listened to her words, I felt only disappointment that we'd be having sprouts for supper.

When mum returned, much later, I was awake in our room and my tummy hurt. I'd been whispering my secrets to the oak tree that loitered outside the window but when I heard her open the door I burrowed under the blankets and closed my eyes. She smelt different now, the fruity scent gone and replaced by an odour that was musky and pungent.

I snatched a peek as she climbed over me to get into bed

and saw how swollen her lips were, as if she'd put too much of her red lipstick on without a mirror's guidance. Her neck was a swirl of blotches and she was smiling to herself. She looked happy.

I've borrowed the bones of my mother's recollections and fleshed them out with my own. Are they true? I can remember how mum smelt, both before and after her assignation with my father, and I remember the sting of his hair cutting into the flesh of my hands as I held on for dear life and for Granny Ivy. But was it real?

Because, you see, I can also remember screaming, spinning across the bedroom when I was about six as a spider thrashed around in the knots of my hair. And that didn't actually happen, according to mum. Well, it did happen, but to her when she was a child, not to me. She'd told me about it and I'd internalised the incident and made it my own. Memory's a trickster like that, isn't it? We all have a habit of rewriting our histories, donning and shedding layers as it suits us and believing every version. I'm no different, so consider yourself warned.

I was nine when my father disappeared, never to be heard of again. I attacked him twice more in the intervening five years, or so I'm told.

One of those times was at a picnic. Allegedly. I'm slightly dubious about this one as I don't remember a thing. Not even a smell. According to mum she'd spent ages persuading Lawrence to give me another chance and so we all went on a picnic, like a proper family. Jolly decent of him. He passed me a sandwich and I leaned in and bit his hand with my sharp little teeth. I growled. He had to have a tetanus shot.

Five stitches. He had to have five bloody stitches!

15

The other time I do remember but that doesn't make it true. He was stood at the front gate, waiting, while my mum hurled herself around the bathroom with hairbrush and mascara. His car filled the lane and was the colour of cherries a day before they've reached their peak. I wanted to pat the bonnet but didn't want to speak to him. I started to trot down the path, pretending to be a horse, and then broke into a canter and then a full-on gallop. Beds of forget-me-nots collided into one solid blur of colour as I raced down the path and prepared to jump the hurdle. Was I trying to skip past him and get to the car? Who knows? Either way, no matter how pure my intentions, I whinnied and butted him square in the stomach and he folded in half and clung to me to avoid falling over. His breath against my cheek thick and wet with pain.

After that he didn't even get out of the car when he came to collect my mum. He just hit the horn and kept the engine running. Sometimes his gaze would find mine as I peeped from the kitchen window, and he'd nod and raise a hand. I'd nod back and show those sharp little teeth in a grin and he'd lower his hand to his lap and look away. I knew then that he'd be massaging the scar I'd given him and the car's interior would echo with the battle cry that I'd shrieked into his stomach.

Has my mother ever forgiven me for his disappearance? Is there a chance she ever will? I know there are times when she blames me entirely for it.

Those times when she doesn't speak are the worst.

Every day since my return to the island, I see her strain towards the window, lumber from foot to foot until she gets too tired to stand, her varicose veins pushing through her tights like a nest of slow-worms, and I want to kneel behind her on the rug and see her as she used to be. My young, beautiful mother, in her gauzy dresses and her ridiculous heels. My magical mother, who could disappear without even needing a puff of smoke.

She refuses to move from this house. Even after Granny Ivy died and left behind plump pensions and insurance policies, she wouldn't even book a week's holiday to the mainland. You see, she believes he will come back for her. Just like old times. He'll appear in the lane in his magnificent motorcar and she'll lift up her skirts and run to him.

She knows that there are such things as telephone directories and he could track her down if he wanted to, but deep inside her, flailing for air beneath the hope and the gin, is the belief that if she made it too hard for him then he just wouldn't bother. She needs to stay right here, right where he can find her without any effort.

What he'd make of me being here as well I can only imagine. The poor sod, to finally return after an absence of seventeen years, certain that, by now, I must *surely* have gone. Only to find me once more narrowing my eyes at him over the threshold as I help mum up from her chair and out of her slippers.

I wouldn't be here at all if she hadn't needed me. I did actually leave Spur and was making a fairly decent stab at adulthood all by myself on the mainland when she called me back. Or rather Tommy did. He'd dropped by with some eggs and found her at the bottom of the stairs, twisted and spiky with broken bones. She'd been lying there for most of the afternoon, inching a tortured route across the hallway. Tommy thinks she'd been trying to reach the phone but I reckon it was more likely the bottle of gin on the dresser in the kitchen.

When he phoned from the hospital with his catalogue of injuries – *concussion, broken wrist and elbow. Cracked ribs as well. She can't manage by herself, love, you need to be with her* –

I asked for time off from the cafe and agreed to come home. Just for a while, just until she could be safely left alone. It didn't take long to pack a bag and put all the plants out in the back garden to fend for themselves. The rent was taken care of for the next month and thanks to Granny Ivy I had savings to fall back on. There was nothing else to stop me. And once I'd committed I suddenly yearned for that sense of snugness only living on the island had ever given me. Swaddled by sea on all sides, safe.

To be honest I wanted to see her again, spend some time with her. Maybe even ask some questions. I've become sentimental lately, preoccupied with the past. I want to pick through that collision of gristle and genes that links the generations, try to make some sense of it. And that means I'll need to know something about him. My father.

I've spent my life refusing all knowledge of him, as if I could somehow be tainted by the familiarity. I don't even have a clear memory of what he looked like anymore because there are no photographs of him. It's only lately that I've come to accept, though grudgingly, that he had just as much to do with forming the person I am as my mother did.

We're doing okay actually. Me and mum. Since my return she's discovered gratitude and a sense of humour, and so we laugh a lot. It's generally barbed laughter, and at the other's expense, but that's how we both are.

Or how we've become.

*

Today she's indulging one of her bad, sad moods and she got at the gin while I was out watching the morning ferry from the mainland come into harbour. We have a rule that generally

18

works: I won't try to stop her drinking and she won't try to pour it down her throat before dinnertime. I cheat a little, I have to confess, because I keep all of the alcohol on the top shelf of the kitchen cupboard so she'd be hard pushed to reach it without my saying so, and I can't see her scaling the cabinets unaided. But this morning she outmanoeuvred me somehow. Maybe after lunch I'll slick the kitchen counters with olive oil or tie her to her chair while she's sleeping it off.

'Oh, Fern, I still can't believe he just upped and left us,' she whispers to me as I try to wrestle the glass from her. She's as devastated as ever she was, and I'm a little in awe of a love so splintering that it can still hurt her this much. I give her a hug and then twist the glass out of her grasp. She lunges for it, arm flapping in its sling, and I drink down the contents quickly. Wince at the strength of the barely-mixed spirit.

'Gone. And no more until dinner. Remember your promise, mum.'

As I turn to leave she kicks out with a bloated foot and catches me on the ankle. I almost laugh despite the sting of it. 'Hey. That bloody hurt.'

'It's all your fault. You ruined everything. You and your bloody grandmother. You never wanted me to be happy.'

She tries to heave herself out of her chair but alcohol and anguish conspire to turn her bones to rubber. I hover a wary couple of feet away and watch her struggle and my irritation bleeds into pity. Again. But I won't move any closer, not just yet. She hasn't exhausted the limit of her pain and anger.

'You drove him away, with your nasty, spiteful temper. I thought we could be a family. Once I had you I thought it would all be different. And maybe it would have been if you'd only behaved like a proper daughter, given him a reason to want to come back.'

I cradle the glass to my chest and try to remember how fragile she is. Try to remember that this is not forever. Then I put the glass down.

'You weren't exactly a great mother, if memory serves.'

She swipes at me again, carves a shaky path through the dust motes dawdling in the sunlight. I laugh with bitter pleasure and dance backwards. 'Missed.'

Mum grunts and hunches on the edge of her chair, swaying. She looks as if she's about to topple right off it. 'I did my best. But you were impossible. Couldn't be trusted to behave like a normal little girl. And as for your grandmother…'

I pick up the glass and turn to go. 'Leave her alone. She practically raised me.'

Her voice rises. 'You were nothing but her puppet. You know she was a witch. She used you to break us up. Turned you feral every time he came near you.'

Sweat studs her upper lip and her cheeks are purpled with distress.

'What can I say to that, mum? Apart from … Oh no, it's come back. The feral beast has come back.'

I claw the air and contort my face, wiggle my tongue at her. After a second's prim silence she titters grudgingly and flaps her good hand at me. 'Don't mock me, Fern.'

I lean over her and kiss her damp forehead. 'As if I ever would.'

As I butter bread in the kitchen I can feel the delicate change of pressure in the house that means she's either asleep or groping towards it. I sit at the table and eat her share of sandwiches as well as mine, look around me at the room. Each mark and stain tags a memory. The cracked tiles by the cooker are twenty years old, but the look on Granny Ivy's face when she dropped her stew pot after I'd crept up on her makes me shiver even now.

That burnt patch on the work surface is still livid, a perfect circle scorched into the wood by the bottom of a pan when mum tried to fry eggs and drink gin at the same time. This house is as familiar to me as the inside of my own skull.

The phone starts to ring as I'm washing up and I jump and drop my plate into the sink, creating a wave that splashes over the side and onto my jeans. I'll never get used to the presence of a telephone in this house. As I wipe my hands dry I try to remember exactly when mum got it. It can't have been that long before I left home. Now when the phone sounds she doesn't even bother to answer it. She'd surrendered her fantasies when she had it installed, had probably known then that taking an active step towards embracing her life would only highlight its inadequacies. It's far safer to be passive, to wait at the window and hope. Against her better judgement and the rules she lived her life by, she let the phone intrude on this and then she sat and watched it day after day, scooping it up occasionally to check the dial tone, before finally accepting that though it may ring, it would never ring for her.

I prod mum awake in the late afternoon and refuse to let her have any more to drink until she's eaten some soup. The television distracts her from her sulk and she spoons up her meal while she watches the early news bulletin and tuts gloomily at the sorry state of the world beyond her front door. She pats the faded velvet of her armchair with each fresh piece of news, as if to congratulate herself on her good sense in having narrowed her existence to this handful of rooms.

'Silly man,' she says to herself. 'Wearing that tie with those trousers. Lawrence would never do that. He's never anything but smartly dressed.'

Then she flinches as she remembers and stares down into her soup, using her spoon to swirl the liquid around the bowl.

As I pull her out of her chair to walk the obligatory post-meal lap of the room, she reaches to stroke my hair.

'Are you okay, love?' she asks. 'You look sad.'

Her concern leaves me speechless. I'm not used to such sensitivity from her. Sarcasm deserts me momentarily so I rush out of the room with her stained napkin and run it under the taps, lean over the sink and watch it darken and shift beneath the push of the water. Something about my stance, or the gape of the plughole, makes me want to retch and I abandon the cloth and return to the living room with two big tumblers.

Mum's back in her chair and I suspect that she cut corners on her circuit. Probably did a quick shuffle on the spot and called it quits. The television has been switched off and she's sitting with her hands folded in her lap, watching the door. I pass her one of the glasses and watch as she takes a greedy gulp then scowls at me.

'Very bloody funny. This is soda water.'

'Oops, sorry.' I swap her glass for mine and smirk as she sips at it cautiously, then more deeply. 'That better?'

'Much better. Bit too much tonic for my liking but I won't complain.'

'Well, amen to that small mercy.' I raise my glass to her and she smiles. She looks lovely for a second, but then she puckers her lips for another go at her drink.

'You always were cheeky,' she observes. 'From the moment you could speak, always so quick with the backchat and the sarcasm. I worried that you'd never get a man to warm to you, you were that prickly. And it looks like I was right.'

She studies me expectantly. I gaze at the wall and open my

mouth as if to speak, then shut it again. I can feel her rising frustration and when she starts to huff I laugh and respond.

'Okay, mum, what do you want to know? Did I ever manage to attract a man? But what if I'm not interested in men, did you ever think of that?'

She looks so confused I want to take it back. It's easy to forget how insular, how innocent, she can be. I rush to fill the silence before she asks me to clarify.

'You want to know if there have been men? Yes, mum, of course there have. I remember a particularly nice one called Mark in my first term at university, and an absolute bastard who two-timed me in my final year. He lasted longer than he should have done, but he was fun in a way. And there've been lots since then, just please don't ask me to do a head count.'

She still looks confused. 'But, Fern, weren't any of them special? Don't you want to get married?'

I roll my eyes at her but she's got her nose buried in her glass and doesn't see.

'I'm not like you, mum. You mated for life, but that sort of 'always and forever, till the end of time' stuff doesn't sit well on some people. It can make them twitchy. It can make them leave.'

Her response is immediate and reflexive, her loyalty as touching as it is misplaced.

'Don't speak about your father like that.'

She takes another gulp at her gin to soothe herself. I cast around to change the subject and am about to speak when she continues. 'You know, there's nothing wrong with true love, Fern. It shouldn't scare you. Do you have someone special right now?'

She brightens immediately at my hesitation. 'Ooh, you have as well. Tell me about him. What's his name? How long have you been seeing him? What does he do?'

I can't help but grin at her excitement. 'His name's Rick and we've been together a while. But I'm not taking it too seriously.' I look away from her, to the clock above the mantle. The evening ferry will be docking soon.

'Why not?' she asks. 'Rick's a lovely name. I'm sure he's lovely. Maybe he's the one? The one that'll get you to settle down.'

I shift against the lumpy cushions and hiss breath through my teeth. 'For god's sake, I'm not like you, mum. I'm not.'

I don't know who's getting more uptight here. She frowns but looks almost smug as she wriggles in her chair and finishes her drink. 'It's in your genes, love. There's nothing you can do about it.'

She hands me her glass for a refill. 'So. Tell me everything about him. Why don't you invite him to stay here with us one weekend? I think I'd like to meet this Rick.'

I stand and tilt my head towards the window, my body tense as if I'm listening to or seeing something denied to her. And she immediately swivels and strains, and forgets.

'What? What is it? Is it a car? Is it stopping?'

Cruel, I know, but it works every time.

A Torn Scrap Of Dark Blue Handkerchief

When I first saw you, I had the sun in my eyes. You shone around the edges, a fireball of a man. In the moments it took me to focus on your centre, I'd absorbed you completely. My pores plugged by your smile. You made me shy.

You watched me dance, wild and uncoordinated and my hair vivid with sweat, and you fell in love with me instantly, knelt at my feet and pressed your handkerchief to my scratched knees as gently as you would later press your lips there.

I remade myself in tune to your blinks, your frowns, your glances away from me and then back. I read your needs as they soared across your face, and I carved myself anew again and again, hacking at the rough clay of my personality and re-sculpting, re-forming, without you even needing to speak.

I became like one of those tiny ballerinas who unfold from the raised lid of a jewellery box and perform for as long as needed. Do you ever wonder what happens to them once the lid is closed? Do they continue to swoop and swirl? Limbs gliding through the cramped space below the polished wood. Eyes wide and searching for the cracks that will bring the light. Buried alive.

You believed that we were special, set apart from other lovers, and I took it upon myself to ensure that we never had that moment. That moment when two people in love suddenly see each other, without the twin deceits of passion and hope obscuring the view, and they falter and move on but are never quite the same.

Think of a pressed flower between the pages of a book; it's still recognisable, it looks like what it is, but it's lost the freshness, the essence that once it had. You still keep it, it still triggers the fond memories that led to its capture and crush, but it's no longer the perfect thing it was.

It's the same with love. I never thought to ask what our future would be. Never thought to establish whether you would take me away from this island and introduce me to the world I'd been waiting my whole life to meet. I thought that would be obvious.

You thought your intention, to keep what we had away from the complications of your life, keep me pure, was just as obvious, and so we never talked about any of it until it was too late.

My breakfast splashed around the toilet bowl. My womb no longer a hollow den.

Do you remember those nights when you stretched out on your stomach on the grass beneath the oak and I tapped out tunes up and down your spine? You guessed wrong every time. Every time. Do you remember that?

2

I was ten the first time my mum went away 'for a break' and came back with a grimace so vague and so permanently fixed that it didn't slip even when she was asleep. I still see shades of it now, just occasionally, when she's overtired or overwrought. Violet creases chase each other around her mouth as her face corrugates and sinks. I hate it. I turn away and start to hum silly little childish tunes.

Every night, I'd lie in the bed we shared and curl up as far from her as I could get, terrified of that bland sadness and the emptiness behind it. Knowing that if I turned around and peered through the darkness, I'd see the glisten of moonlight reflected in her staring eyes. I started having nightmares.

Men with wolves' heads and red wellington boots pursued me through deserted streets. My mum's face high among the stars called for me to fly up to her, only I couldn't get my feet to leave the ground. A runaway car with no driver tipped me off the edge of the world, hurtling me through layers of nothingness.

I began to wet the bed, waking the next day chilled and

ashamed. Mum would yawn and roll into the damp sheets, hands pressed hard against her flickering, wayward eyelids.

What time is it, Fern? It can't be morning already. Wake me in an hour.

Granny Ivy agreed to let me have the tiny spare bedroom, the one Grandfather Edgar had died in. I whimpered and weighed the options and concluded that the dead would haunt me less than the living. I washed the sheets through three times to get rid of any ghostly traces and then moved out of the room that had been my mum's since she was a child, and into my first proper bedroom.

And the bed-wetting stopped.

I saved my pocket money and took a bus into town to buy yellow paint from Woolworth's. How impressed my mum would be when she heard I'd caught a bus all by myself. But the paint was too thin, the walls too vast, and the old green bled through the delicate primrose like nicotine-stained handprints. I cut pictures of kittens and cute dormice from school friend's magazines to cover the ugly blotches, and delighted in the shiny jostle of colour.

I missed the scratch and sigh of the old oak tree waving its branches at me, the whisper of its leaves, but I loved my new pink curtains, made from one of mum's cast-off dresses. They did nothing to block the light but they quivered in the breeze as if they were dancing with the window frames.

I wanted mum to notice my absence. Maybe even miss the warmth and wriggle of my body next to hers in the night, but she never commented on it. At bedtime, when Granny Ivy looked pointedly from the mantelpiece clock to me and put her sewing aside, I'd haul myself to my feet, trail schoolwork and sighs, and fuss over my night time routine. Satchel left packed and ready by the back door, teeth cleaned, clothes neatly folded, and then a return to the front room for goodnight kisses. Waiting for some words of acknowledgement to accompany the scouring-pad scrape of mum's chapped lips against my forehead.

Haven't you grown up, Fern, such a big girl in your very own bedroom!

Always waiting.

Sometimes, when I couldn't sleep, I'd slide out of bed and tiptoe down the hall. As quiet as a cloud past Granny Ivy's closed bedroom door, and then into mum's room. She'd be lying in the scribble of shadows the oak tree conjured in the moonlight and threw across the bed. She never remembered to shut her curtains anymore. Her window wide open, even on the coldest nights. Sometimes she'd shiver uncontrollably in her sleep. I'd struggle with the old wood, try to shut the night out, and sometimes slip into bed beside her to warm her up. I never fell asleep but would wait until she unfolded with the heat I wrapped her in and then I'd tuck her up, covers pulled to her chin, and tiptoe back to my room.

Those were the times I prefer to remember. Not the other times, the too many times when I stood in the doorway and watched silently as she faced the ceiling and cried without appearing to know she was crying. Tears in jagged trails across her cheekbones. Or when she gasped and sat up in response to the tiny noise of my entrance, stared at me with her arms half raised, palms glowing a welcome through the dim air, blinked slowly and then collapsed back against the pillows and turned her head away.

Thoughts of those times pull my scalp tight and prickly across my skull and make me wish that this were over now, that I were returned to my previous life, away from this island and this house, to a place where I am wanted, just for being me.

After a while mum's twitch faded, and she blinked more. How long did it take? Weeks? Months? Anyway, I kept my mouth shut and hoped that wouldn't mean I'd have to move back in with her. My legs crossed at the very thought, my bladder throbbed with anxiety. But Granny Ivy seemed happy with the current sleeping arrangements.

There's no point chopping and changing. You'd only need to shift again the next time.

The next time? I hadn't realised mum's little holidays would be a regular thing.

Over the next couple of years I got to recognise the signs that precipitated one of her trips away. The high, thin sound she made after hours spent rubbing the front window clean of any trace of grime, only to mist it immediately with her breath. The way she cradled her keepsake box, refused to put it aside even at the meal table, stroking its crooked clasp until sores eventually silvered her hands with bracelets of scars. The precision with which she measured her steps from bedroom to bathroom, or from bedroom to kitchen, muttering the even numbers, humming the odd.

When I knew it was that time again, holiday time, I'd help her pack her weekend bag in preparation, pick out pretty dresses and high-heeled shoes that would later mysteriously disappear and be replaced with trousers and blouses, pairs of thick socks. She never sent a postcard or brought a souvenir back, and I never stopped hoping that she would.

30

I know now where she disappeared to and maybe a part of me even then had a sense of how broken she was. Every time we waved her off the air smelt brittle and acrid, as if a storm were about to spill its fury over my head. The adults conversed mechanically and smiled with their mouths and I covered my nose, staring up at the sky and waiting for the first judder of lightning to pierce the blue. Nudged into good manners, I'd skip after the taxi as it rolled slowly down the lane, waving at Tommy as he sat behind the wheel, smoking and tooting his horn, while mum sorted frantically through the contents of her handbag and didn't look up.

Granny Ivy would stand by the gate and wait for me to walk limply back to her. She'd put an arm around me, quickly, all the while focused on something in the distance. She'd squeeze me painfully and then let me go, almost pushing me away, then she'd sniff and fumble for a handkerchief.

Just the two of us again, Fern. But we won't make a fuss about it. Shall I fry us some potatoes for supper?

Those lonely evenings sat across from each other, heaping cushions onto the empty chair to give the illusion of solidity, of substance. At a glance, unfocused, there could be three of us in the room. Granny Ivy lit candles and whispered over her sewing, fingering her silk bag of jewels. I'd believed they were boiled sweets when I was younger and had cracked a tooth on a sticky sliver of jasper. Granny Ivy whispered and tied the tiniest knots into a piece of silver thread, dribbled wax along its length, and when I went to bed at night I slid my hand under my pillow and cupped the chunks of tourmaline that had been left there.

Mum doesn't like to talk about those times and I know that

it must have crucified her to be separated from home, and her vigil. I only realised years later that she had to leave Spur altogether and travel to the hospital on Sorel, the next island over. After the car had taken her away but before the machine's crackle and spark pulsed tranquillity through her brain, flushing her clean of despair, she must have been frantic. Frantic to remain where she was, where my father could find her. And maybe even frantic to stay with us, no matter how little she showed it.

And so it would go on. The absence, the empty room at the end of the hall. The return of the half-mother, her face a wincing mask and her soul once more straitjacketed into submission.

*

The rain has stopped now and the garden is rinsed with citric tones. I settle mum into one of the deck chairs with a blanket and a tiny gin and tonic (our compromise – fresh air in exchange for a pre-dinner drink), and start to collect the dead leaves. As soon as I've raked a decent enough pile of them the wind tugs them loose and scatters them around my feet. Mum points and laughs and I grin over at her. This is as good a way as any to while away the day.

'Will you find him for me?' she asks suddenly. 'Lawrence?'

I stop and lean on the rake. 'Why now?'

'Because I'm tired out. I'm tired of missing him. And because I want him to see you, the woman you've become.'

I drop the rake and walk over to her. 'Yes, but why now, after all this time? Why not right after he disappeared, or when Granny Ivy died, or when I left home? Why now, when it will only hurt you more than you can handle?'

She stares past me at the oak tree. One of its leaves has flung itself, damp and filmy, against my leg, and I stoop to flick it off.

'What do you think will happen, mum? I'll find him, he'll show up here, hold you in his arms and proclaim undying love? He's had plenty of opportunities to do that over the years and he hasn't taken any of them. It's time to accept that he's not coming back.'

I expect her to start crying. I want her to start crying. She looks at me for a solemn moment and then reaches to pat my cheek. 'You're still so full of anger towards him, aren't you? When you get like this you're the spit of your grandmother. She'd be proud of you.'

She smiles at the point she's scored and tips her nose into her glass. I breathe through my nostrils to calm myself down and rub at the pulpy imprint the oak leaf has left on my jeans.

'Can't you just leave her memory alone, please? She might have had her faults …'

Mum snorts through a mouthful of gin and starts to choke. I stand and watch, taking a spiteful pleasure in her discomfort, but then move to pull her forward and thump her between the shoulder blades.

'Well,' I say, jolting her back and forth, 'what does that tell you? The man upstairs clearly doesn't like you bad-mouthing one of his flock.'

She points at the ground and wipes her mouth with her sleeve. 'The man downstairs, Fern. Believe me, it'll be the man downstairs.'

I acknowledge the joke with a tight lip-twitch and settle on the ground by her feet.

'But, mum, what if he doesn't want to know? What if he's dead, did you ever think of that? Or what if he takes one look at my face and hurls himself screaming through the nearest window? You do see that there isn't going to be a happy ending, don't you?'

She rests her hand on the top of my head and suddenly I'm my four-year-old self again, trapped beneath my father's reluctant palm. I force myself not to shrug her off. She sighs and tangles her fingers into my hair and we sit for a while in silence. I almost start to doze but then her hand tightens on my scalp and I jerk away. Her fingers collapse through the air and into her lap and she sniffs and looks down, fumbles through her coat pockets for her handkerchief. Her eyes have taken on the glassy sheen of marbles left out in the rain.

'Oh, Fern, I miss him.'

I rub her shin as she wipes at her face and I make soothing noises through closed lips. I'm determined not to give in. I know I'm right.

Her shoulders start to heave and she knuckles the shabby brown handkerchief brutally into her eye sockets. I'm scared that she'll start making that high, thin sound from my childhood.

'Okay, I'll do it. I'll look for him.'

I regret it immediately, but she lowers her handkerchief and presses her sodden cheek to mine and my resentment is shot through with relief that she's smiling again.

'You'd better give me a starting point,' I say. 'Last known address. I can go to the library tomorrow after I've taken you to the hospital. It's not going to be easy, though, if he's not from Spur or Sorel.'

She bites at the skin of her index finger, worrying at it. 'I don't have an address. But he wasn't an islander. I'm sure he lived on the mainland.'

'Okay, well where did he work?'

She mumbles something I don't catch through a mouthful of fingertip and I ask her to repeat it.

'There's nothing, Fern. Nothing relevant anyway.'

She won't meet my eyes. I laugh and shake my head. I'd always assumed that my ignorance in all things related to my father was down to my own denial of him, my wilful deafness whenever his name was mentioned. 'But that's ridiculous. You can't have a relationship as all-consuming as yours was and not know even simple things about him.'

She starts scratching at the stitches in her handkerchief, getting her thumbnail into a loose one and teasing it away from the fabric. The handkerchief starts to pucker, curling in on itself like a dying woodlouse. We both watch and I wait for her to respond.

Once she's sawed the thread completely with her sharp nails she smoothes the handkerchief flat across her knees, nods down at it. There's something bitter about the movement, the accompanying wry smile.

'I don't suppose this will be any help? It's his. There's nothing else really. I only knew a few things about him for certain, Fern, he preferred it that way. He didn't even like having his photograph taken. When we were together it was just about the two of us. No past, no future, no baggage.'

This is why I stayed away for so many years. This knowledge that my very existence is no more than *baggage*, an offshoot from the trunk of her main love. And this is why I've always shrugged her off whenever she's wanted to talk about him. The anger is always there, just below the surface, and it hurts us both.

'Bullshit you were just two people. You shared a child together. Don't tell me you were happy with that arrangement, tucked away in your toy box until he was ready to take you out to play.'

'It wasn't like that. I can't explain it to you in a way that would make you understand. He loved me …'

I laugh at her. Furious. Cruel. 'What, every third Thursday and alternate bank holidays? He couldn't possibly squeeze any more love for you than that?'

She catches one of my hands and holds on. Presses it hard. 'You know he was married. It wasn't that easy.'

I try to turn away. 'Easy for who? I can't imagine it was a struggle for him.'

'Don't, Fern. He loved me. He loved us both.'

Bile washes sour at the back of my throat. I cover my mouth, speak through my palm. '*Us both?* Are you talking about me and you, or you and her? Did he keep pictures of his proper family in his wallet, mum? Did you talk about them?'

She closes her eyes and rubs at her cheek. She looks exhausted. I'm suddenly aware of the lateness of the afternoon, the chill crawling up from the grass. I gently tug my hand from hers but she scrabbles to retrieve it, pressing it to her chest. We make an awkward tableau, stiff and shivering in the sunlight, our faces blank with pain.

Her words are whispered. 'I know I didn't ever put you first, Fern, and I'm sorry. Really I am. We never talked about his wife. He never apologised for it and I never tried to make him feel guilty. Not even when you came along.'

I clear my throat and reach to pick up her glass and book. 'Well, that's a relief, just as long as he wasn't made to feel bad.'

If she's bothered by my sarcasm she doesn't show it. I haul her onto her feet and steady her across the lawn. Her body quivers beneath my grip and I pause by the oak. 'Are you really sure you want me to do this, mum? It's been a long time and things aren't going to be the same.'

She gropes with her good arm to pat the old tree and smiles, more at it than at me. 'I want this. I'll be fine, darling.'

Tommy comes to the back door while I'm cooking dinner. I meet him on the step and give him a hug. He's got a lot thinner but his arms around me feel as thick and ropey as they ever did. When I was young I used to be able to lace my fingers around one of his forearms and swing myself off the ground, and know that he would hold my weight.

He kisses the top of my head and then steps away to look at me properly. 'You look great, love, really well. I'm so glad you came back to look after your mum. How is she?'

I steer him down the path a little way. 'She's having a nap at the moment. Do you want me to wake her?'

He shakes his head. 'No, leave her be. I just popped by to say hello and see how she is. How you both are. It's been so long since you visited. Is it good to be home?'

I grimace at him. 'I wouldn't go that far. It feels strange. Mum's just the same though.'

He laughs at that, but distractedly. 'Do you think so? I've been worried about her for a while. She's more absentminded these days. Seems to be collapsing the past into the present, forgetting herself.'

'It's probably the drink,' I say briskly. 'Though she's asked me to look for him. My dad. And I said I would.' My voice is sharper than I intended. Challenging.

He nods and looks away. 'Maybe it'll help her to know what happened.'

We stand in silence for a while and I pity him his hopeless

love for my mum. I'd always hoped she'd pity him too, turn to him for comfort and find some kind of contentment. But lukewarm loving never worked for her. And maybe the situation suits him too. Maybe, like her, he'd rather love a cipher, an absent figure, than sacrifice the dream to crinkled skin over the breakfast table and petty irritations.

He hugs me again and makes to leave. 'Didn't I see you at the dock yesterday?' he asks. 'I'm sure it was you. Parked up on the headland at the beauty spot, looking out to sea through a pair of binoculars. I waved.'

I shrug and look away. 'Yes, it could have been me. I like to watch the ferries come in and out.'

He raises my head with a hand under my chin and winks at me. 'I'll be back soon, kid. Give your mother my best. Look after her for me.'

Mum and I spend the evening playing rummy and I pour her a few generous drinks, win every game. She shakes her head at me as I crow with triumph and scoop another pile of coins onto my lap.

'You should be ashamed of yourself, Fern. Taking advantage of my weakness.'

I tip my head towards her near empty glass. 'Another one?'

'Oh, yes please.'

'Okay, shuffle and deal and I'll be back in a sec.'

My legs and chest stop performing their usual functions just as I'm mixing the drinks and I'm on the floor and sobbing before I know what's happened. I can barely breathe. I stretch out, kick the door closed, crawl under the table and surrender myself. I have no idea why I'm crying, or for whom, so I settle on Granny Ivy. I conjure up her voice, the smell of her apron, the bony clasp of her hand, and let myself miss her.

The phone starts to shrill from its place on the sideboard, pulses of sound that fill the pauses between sobs. Impatience filters through from the front room and I stagger to my feet, call out to forestall any appearance.

'Just rescuing a moth, mum, be through in a minute.'

I can hear her muttering to herself as I splash water on my face and then collect the glasses. She's at least two drinks past the mellow stage.

'It's okay, panic over. There you go.'

I sit down in the armchair and put her drink on the coffee table. Her mouth's twisted in on itself like a poisoned rosebud, but then she peers at me and takes in the swollen eyelids and the rose blooms and blossoms.

'Oh, Fern. What happened?'

'It died. The moth. It was caught up in a cobweb and I crushed it trying to get it free.'

'I'm sorry to hear that,' she says slowly. 'Was that the phone I heard? Who was it? Was it Rick?'

I shake my head and reach for my glass. We sip for a moment in silence and she watches me as if she's about to say, or ask, something else. I'm in no mood for a heart to heart. I pick up my cards, look them over, and nod towards her purse.

'I think you'd better crack open the notes, mum. I'm upping the stakes and coins just aren't going to cut it.'

She fumbles through the worn compartments and starts to count her remaining funds. 'You'll have the shirt off my back, you evil girl. We'd better go to the bank tomorrow after you've taken me to the hospital. Replenish my supply.'

But she's smiling.

A Clipped Square From The Top Of A Cigarette Box

Afterwards. After you'd lain on me in the back seat of your car, covered me with your hands, blocked out the moon and the stars until the night narrowed to just the skin of your neck – afterwards – I remembered my mother's words.

Drowsy with joy and desperate to prove her wrong, so sure that she would be wrong, I laughed as I asked you if you were married, and didn't understand why you weren't laughing too.

You hissed smoke out between your teeth and glanced at me. Glanced away.

I think other women would have wanted to know everything then. Every detail of every aspect of this other life. Gorged themselves on the pain of it until they were plump and ripe with its awfulness. Carried it around with them forever afterwards, so carefully, like a vase too big and too heavy, too full of water. Dripping its load no matter how delicately they cradled it.

They'd have wanted to know everything.

Do you wind her hair into a rope, to cling to as you climb her body? Did you buy two sets of camisoles in silver satin, one for each of us? When you see me wearing mine, in the subtle confusion of night, do you mistake me for her?

Does she cover her mouth when she laughs, or does she throw her head back and show the world her teeth? Do you watch her when she sleeps, and will yourself into her dreams?

Does she stride across the earth with long, confident steps, dance beneath the hectic sky during a summer storm, or does she take your arm and lean into you? Does she believe in ghosts, and fairies, and monsters?

Does she know about us? Does she?
Does she ever think about me?

I slid onto your knees, took your chin gently in the palm of my hand, and turned your head. We looked at each other and I peeped between your parted lips, saw the confession squatting on your tongue. The need to press words like bruises onto me. I kissed that need from your mouth, and then I smiled. I laughed. And I felt so tremendously happy.

You wouldn't understand that. The elation. The relief. So crooked, so twisted, when I say it aloud. But that kiss was a farewell to all the harsh mornings that would never be. Your wrinkles written on your face and crumbs around your mouth. Turning your pillow over with discreet pity, to bury your fallen hair. Looking down at my hands in the sink, reddened and rough from soap powder, and wrapped around your underpants. That future was no longer mine to experience.

And so I laughed with a joy that came from being given the freedom to love you outside reality, as it were. In a magical place of half-light and shadows. A place you would return to again and again and find me waiting for you, unchanged and unmarked. Fingers cupped around the flame of what we shared, keeping it bright and steady. Keeping it safe.

And, of course, there was our child. Our Fern. Already curled inside me, the size and shape of a sweet pea blossom. My secret to share.

I'm not saying that I could manage to plumb those depths of joy and faith as deeply ever again, or even at all. Because I loved you. Because of course I wanted it all. I wanted the wrinkles and the fallen hair and the hands red and raw. And then I didn't. And that's how it's been ever since that night; the relief and contentment followed so swiftly behind by the need and the longing that I can barely separate the push and pull of it all.

I held your face between my palms and I kissed you, and I laughed, and we never spoke about it. Not once. I didn't ask you to confirm it, because I didn't need to. I'd seen it in your mouth.

I think you always regretted that, and maybe you even resented it a little. I never gave you a chance to explain, did I? You wanted the opportunity to confess and excuse, make promises and then retract them, and I denied you that.

But what I did, I did for us, and I did for me. I still believe that was right. Would it have helped me to see the photographs of your home, to imagine your heart beating against her spine through the night, to shout and cry and call you names?

It wouldn't have changed anything.

But what if it had? What if all you'd needed was for me to imprison you with words, not set you free with silence?

3

I was twelve when Granny Ivy died and gave herself the ultimate final say during a huge row with my mother. Mum was furious with her for months afterwards. I was furious with mum.

I was on the fringes of the row though not part of it, curled in the very same armchair that mum now glowers from every night and claims didn't even exist then. She's wrong about that, I know she is.

I was huddled in my dressing gown and slippers, hands wrapped over my head as spite arced across the living room in thin, sharp slivers. Words spat like pins. They dug through skin and flesh until they found my granny's core and pierced it. She flung her hand out – To me? To mum? – and then plummeted to the floor, apron fluttering. A peace flag raised too late.

The memory does make me pause when mum and I are in the middle of one of our insult hurling competitions, and for a second, as I look at her across the jagged pieces of all the things I wish I'd never said, I see in her pupils the tiny twin images of my granny's felled body. And, though mum would never admit it, I know she looks at me and sees the same thing.

I massaged Granny Ivy's stricken heart, cradled it in my hands as it quivered and plunged in the cage of her chest and tried its hardest to fly away from me. Her lips the same grey as her hair. My mother standing over us both.

Don't you dare die! Get back up! Get up!

By the time the ambulance arrived and two solemn men confirmed the worst, my knees were so cramped that I couldn't straighten properly. Mum pulled me to my feet and helped me hobble into the kitchen, where I was sick in the sink until there was nothing left of my porridge. I stayed draped against the slippery porcelain for a while, gripping onto the taps and staring down the plughole, and I wondered how much of Granny Ivy had just come out of my mouth. She'd breathed her last breath deep into me during my clumsy resuscitation, had caught me unawares and filled my lungs full to the brim of her.

For the funeral, held in the local church, mum wore one of her flowery chiffon dresses. Collisions of violet and peach on black satin. I bet she still has that dress somewhere and I know it would look better on me these days than on her. She shivered constantly but I didn't offer her my cardigan. She'd piled her hair up onto her head in a lopsided chignon and looped pearls from Granny Ivy's jewel box around her throat. *Her* jewel box now.

I wore brown, not black. Brown was the colour of decay. The colour of death. The tooth I'd had pulled when I was ten had been brown at the tip, rotting deep inside the soft pink of my mouth.

Seated together in the family pew but not touching, we both pretended deep interest in the vicar's words as he plodded through the service. My eyes were raw and dry, as they had been since Granny Ivy died. Each time I blinked the lids rasped together. When mum started to cry I had to fist my hands together so that I wouldn't poke a finger into each of her eye sockets and gouge out those guilty, healing tears. She wasn't allowed to cry if I couldn't.

The church was full of people who had known my granny in a way I never had and now never would. Customers from the post office who'd received her scribbled remedies for arthritis with their change. Old women, gnarled as tree branches, who swore that they'd survived the long winters only because of my granny's charms and potions. They nudged memories from pew to pew, snatched sentences from their neighbour and passed them back and forth. The vicar may as well not have been there, for all the attention they paid him.

Kindle a candle of purest white, she said ...
And drip wax along the silk, yes, I remember that one ...
No, it was 'drip wax along the skein ...'
Worked a treat, that one did!

They nibbled the ends of pencils and muttered The Toothache Charm to each other, spearing the spell onto paper with their leaden scrawl and slipping it onto my hymnbook when we all stood to pray.

Just in case you ever need it, lovey. Better than aspirin.

As the mourners around me chanted *Our Father*, and mum buried her face in her hands, I stared down at the words, mouthing them as Granny Ivy would once have done.

Find a stone of perfect oval
given hair by weed
or moss.
This shall be your human head.

Wrap it up in paper
soaked overnight in gin
and tie it up with string.

Knot it round and round
And leave it in the full moon's light …

If I covered my ears I could hear her voice inside my head and imagine her standing next to me. I began to chant.

Toothache that resides in me
transfer your woe and let me be.
Toothache, no more make me moan.
Live forever in this stone.

In the quiet that followed the prayer, the reminiscences started up again, and tendon-webbed fingers squeezed my shoulder briefly.

That's the spirit, girl.

Each kindly remembrance forced more air between me and mum and when she uncovered her face and reached out a trembling hand to pat me she had to lean awkwardly and lunge with her arm. I stared ahead and pretended I hadn't noticed.

I started to choke during one of the hymns and had to stumble the length of the chill building. Past all of those stares and then out into the rain. Hands over my mouth, I gasped and struggled with the lump that had lodged inside me, trying to keep it down. The lump that was Granny Ivy's soul, newborn and scrabbling to get free.

Stay with me. Don't go. I'll keep you safe.

Every time I tried to re-enter the church my windpipe would spasm, the lump swelling with panic. We were forced to wait in the dark side porch for the service to end, me and my granny's soul together. I peeked in once and saw her string of pearls exploding away from the warmth of my mum's skin, as if someone, spectral or invisible, had tugged at them. They fired like milky bullets over the coffin, ricocheted off the lectern.

I waited and I circled the gloom. Fractured flagstones zigzagged across the floor, sticky beneath the soles of my shoes. The damp and neglect coated my nostrils with a fine dust, making me sneeze. It clung grittily to the collars of my blouse. If I stayed still I too would start to curl at the edges, bones crumbling within me and collapsing me down onto the filthy floor. I brushed my fingers against the stained walls and then pressed them, lightly, to my tongue. They tasted brown.

A bird's nest spilled from a shelf, oozing feathers, speckled with four tiny skeletons. I stroked each thumbnail-sized head and felt grief bulge briefly behind my eyes as two of them disintegrated beneath the gentle pressure.

The window frame was knobbly with carvings. Letters and numbers, some shapes. A tree; a man, crude and stick-like, but unmistakeable.

And there in the topmost corner, winding around and around itself, a trail of ivy.

Finally, I could cry. I didn't think I'd ever be able to stop.

I met my great-aunt for the first time, after the funeral. The neighbours and Granny Ivy's customers from the post office were gathered in the front room. Muddy footprints and sandwich crumbs all over the carpet. I was outside, alone, under the oak. The rain had stopped but a miserable winter gloom was draped over everything, squeezing the light.

A lady with an umbrella and my granny's stoop came around the side of the house, headed straight towards me. She jerked when I stood up and I realised then that she hadn't been looking for me, wasn't about to fold me to the jut of her upholstered bosom and make it all better. If anything, she looked frankly annoyed to see me there, intruding on whatever she'd been planning. I studied her with open curiosity and the ready affection the young have when they're bereaved and presented with their kin. I was already jumping ahead to fantasies of her moving in with us, donning Granny Ivy's apron and making me pancakes on the weekend. I didn't even think to question why I'd never seen her before, or why my granny had never done more than mention her name in passing. It was enough that she was family, and she was here.

Pins and needles and a mushroom vol-au-vent robbed me of grace and I spluttered a response to her sharp greeting. She stood for a moment in silence and then reluctantly came closer.

So, you're Iris' girl.

I wanted to tell her that that my granny's spirit was safe inside me, was right now snuggled somewhere under my bellybutton, but her face was crisp with disapproval. So I just nodded.

She watched me and sighed impatiently. Tapped the ground with the spike of her umbrella. Fast, fierce little taps.

You take after your mother.

Nobody had ever told me that before. I pondered it with a pang of mingled pride and horror.

She tells me I take after my granny.

The woman bit out laughter, as if it pained her to be amused. She took a step closer.

Then good luck to you. I hadn't spoken to her in years. Ivy. Saw the notice in the paper and thought I'd take the ferry over.

Of course. She lived on Sorel. So Granny Ivy must have come from there originally. To my twelve-year-old self there was something deliciously exotic about not being from this island. And there was so much she could tell me about what Granny Ivy had been like as a young girl. I took an eager step forwards but she took a step back and turned away.

You'd better get inside and deal with your mother. Halfway through a bottle of brandy and singing songs the last time I saw her.

I wiped at my face with the sleeve of my jacket and shook my head.

She doesn't drink. The doctor said she's not allowed to.

The great-aunt lifted one shoulder in a shrug of disinterest. She speared her umbrella tip into the lawn and leaned on it, watching me. I turned and started towards the house, breaking into a run as the sound of mum's singing spilled through the open windows of the front room.

I still wince when I remember that panicked flight across the lawn and the moment when I realised that I wasn't being followed. I slowed and spun around and ran back to the great-aunt, who stood and watched me trip and stumble. It was then that my granny's death became a solid thing. It crouched like a beast in front of me. It roared. My granny was dead.

She was dead and my mother was drunk and I couldn't deal with this by myself.

Please, will you help? You have to stop her.

The great-aunt moved towards me reluctantly, wincing slightly at the hysteria clipping my words. Embarrassed by it.

But she nodded grimly and strode after me, with her shoulders pulled back and her chin up.

I had to drag mum from the front room and her fascinated audience and coax her up the stairs. She lost one of her slingbacks during the struggle to get her up to her bedroom and when I found it the next morning I dropped it into the dustbin and buried it in cigarette ends and potato peelings. Spat on it for good measure. She'd drained all of the dignity out of my granny's funeral and I hated her for that.

The great-aunt tugged plates from reluctant fingers, heaped coats onto laps, and opened all of the downstairs windows to let in the cold air. Within twenty minutes the guests had all gone.

While mum snored her way towards an epic hangover, I made coffee. The great-aunt drank hers standing by the sink, umbrella still hooked over her wrist. I asked her if she'd like to stay for dinner and when she refused I asked her if she'd like to return soon for a visit. The hysteria was edging back in, but this time she wasn't going to be taken hostage.

No, I don't think so. But I'm sure you'll be fine. Say goodbye to your mother for me.

I stood by the window and watched her walk down the path. Her coat captured a gust of wind and billowed out around her, turning her into a giant. She paused to button it up. My arm was raised, ready to wave if she were to turn around. My elbow started to ache but I kept it hoisted in readiness.

That joint still stiffens with remembered rejection, whenever I'm passed over for a job interview or ignored in the street by an old acquaintance. That sudden, sullen throb always makes me think of navy coats, piped with charcoal. In the time it took her to reach the gate and disappear from my life my eager affection had hardened into resentment. If it was just going to be me and mum from now on, if no one else wanted us, then so be it. We'd be fine.

*

It takes ages for mum to be seen by her doctor and the only magazines in the waiting room are tatty copies of *Fast Car* and

Kingpin. There's a couple sitting opposite us who must also be mother and daughter, slouched in their chairs with identical scowls. I nudge mum and angle the toe of my shoe discreetly in their direction. 'I guess both of them. Syphilis. Advanced state in the daughter, just diagnosed in the mother.'

Mum gasps, sniggering behind her fingers, and is still sniggering when she's called in to see the doctor. I stand up to accompany her but she gestures for me to sit back down. 'I can do this by myself, Fern. You wait there and I'll be out soon.'

By the time she returns I've diagnosed most of the waiting patients and am trying to eavesdrop on their conversations to prove myself right. She tugs at my arm to hurry me along. 'There's your bag. Come on, we've got to go to the bank.'

I stretch and stand, taking my time. She keeps thrusting my handbag at me until I take it. 'Come on, Fern. Hurry up.'

I can see a twitch of white behind her, flapping like the underside of a gull's wing. Mum starts to back up, pulling at me, and reverses heavily into the doctor. They both squeak, but she looks the more pained. I grin at her and reach past with my hand out.

'Are you Iris's doctor? Hi, I'm Fern, her daughter. I was hoping to get a chance to speak to you.'

He looks at mum, who hesitates for a moment then nods her acquiescence. As we move into a side room I smile over at her but she cradles her broken wrist and gazes into nothing, ignoring us both. The doctor tries to get her attention and then gives up and turns to me.

I nod and watch his mouth as it forms words. Alcoholic Cardiomyopathy. Increased fatigue and weakness. Radical lifestyle change. Moderate cognitive impairment. Increased anxiety and confusion. Heart failure.

Mum's breathing as if she's asleep and her expression is one of serene disengagement. I try to match my breaths to hers and feel the muscles in my shoulders start to relax. When the doctor pauses I laugh and look from him to mum, and back.

'I don't understand.' I say. 'I know she drinks a bit too much but she's not even fifty. Could the fall down the stairs have done something to her heart?'

The doctor gives me a look that is equal parts incredulity and pity and then turns back to his notes. 'No, Miss Gilbert, it was likely because of her heart that she fell down the stairs. That and the fact that she was drunk.'

I glance around the room while he continues to speak. There's a poster emblazoned with the warning signs of meningitis and I read it through carefully, try to commit the symptoms to memory. You never know when that kind of information might come in handy.

Another has a large, colour picture of a diseased lung, with a cigarette stubbed into it. Wisps of filthy-looking smoke curl all the way up to the top of the poster. I imagine how awful that must have smelt for the photographer taking the shot. How awful for the person who died and donated their organs to science, only to have their shameful lung end up as an ashtray, a warning to others. *No better than it deserved*.

There is silence and I refocus on the doctor. I think he wants some sort of response from me but I'm not sure what he's just said. I glance at mum for help but she's still absorbed in the poster detailing the risks of high cholesterol.

So I smile and nod thoughtfully and tuck my hand into the crook of mum's arm. Her attention snaps back immediately and she swings round to the door. I have to hold onto her jacket to stop her from disappearing as I thank the doctor.

We pass the dour syphilis-ridden pair as we hurry down the corridor and mum nudges me and smirks. I study her face for signs of emotion and see only pleasure in a shared joke.

'Christ, mum, when were you planning on telling me?'

She jabs at the button to call the lift, then takes my wrist and squeezes it. 'I wasn't planning on telling you at all, Fern. It's not your business.'

Outside the bank, I stuff fivers into my purse and give mum back her IOU's. A high-heeled, elegantly dressed middle-aged woman stops and stares. 'Iris?'

We both jump guiltily. Mum peers and stiffens. She smoothes at her fringe. 'Diane? Well. How long has it been? I'm surprised you recognised me, after all these years.'

I think Diane is a little surprised too but she hides it well. She steps close and they embrace awkwardly, mum's silver threaded hair drab beside the other woman's shiny gold. I stand and smile the rigid smile of the excluded.

'And this is my daughter, Fern. Fern, Diane is one of my old friends.'

I give a little wave and murmur a greeting and Diane scans me with interest. She turns back to mum. 'Less of the old, please! God, where do we begin? What happened to your arm? You're looking ... well, how are you?'

I can see mum panicking. She turns to me. 'Aren't we going to be late? For the thing, the appointment?'

I flourish my wrist and frown down at my watch. Twitch the lifeline out of her reach. 'No, we've got plenty of time. You carry on.'

Her eyes narrow. She turns back to Diane who is ready with more questions.

'So, where have you been living? What have you been doing?'

'I've been right here,' Mum tells her. 'I never moved away from the island in the end.'

Diane mimes extravagant surprise and I bristle, immediately regretting my moment of malice. Stooped and shapeless in her coat, hunched over her handbag as if scared it will be stolen from her, mum looks worn and weary, so much older than the woman beside her.

'Really?' Diane raises her eyebrows. 'Out of all of us, I'd have bet you'd be the one to leave. You were always on at us. Then you met that man. So, are any of the old crowd still here? We all used to have such a blast on a Friday night, do you remember? I still think about that.'

Mum pretends to ponder for a moment before answering. Her face has taken on the bland expression of someone steeling themself against hurt. I flick quickly through my childhood memories to try to place this woman but there's no mental index card with her name on it. Before me, then, and before my father. Back when mum had friends. The thought of her once belonging, once having a crowd and a blast is strange, but nice.

She fidgets and bites at her finger. 'No, I don't think there's anyone else left on Spur. Molly went to the mainland with you didn't she, back in sixty-three? And Terry followed a few months later. I lost touch with everyone then. Fern came along in sixty-six, so I got a job at the soap factory and decided to just stay here.'

Diane laughs and covers her mouth with her hand, spraying mirth daintily through her fingers. 'God, I remember the soap factory. We all had jobs there, didn't ever need to use perfume. I'm surprised you gave in and applied, though. Didn't you used to say that it would make you lazy? And what happened with that man you were seeing? Did that last long? We were all convinced he was married.'

I take over as mum flinches slightly. 'Dad, do you mean? Lawrence? He died in a road accident when I was small. Saving a little girl who ran out in front of a lorry. I'm surprised you didn't read about it in the papers at the time, I think it made mainland news. Mum, we really should get you to that thing, that appointment.'

We all stand and bare our teeth at each other. As we walk away, back to the car, mum starts to sniff. 'Why did you say that about your father? She knew you were lying. Did you see how elegant she looked? So ... polished.'

I dig out a tissue and pass it over. 'Polished, my arse. The woman was held together with staples and sticky tape. The poor cow probably hasn't been able to laugh in years in case her ears fall off.'

I glance at her quickly and see that she's looking gratified. 'So, who was she anyway?'

Mum blows her nose loudly and then passes the tissue back to me. 'Just an old childhood friend. She moved away not long after I met your father. All of them did in the end. It's ironic really, I was the only one desperate to get off the island and as it turned out I was the only one who stayed behind.'

The irony seems to fill her legs with concrete and I take her arm as she droops.

As we drive past the church I'm overcome with a sudden urge to visit Granny Ivy's grave. I pull onto the verge and switch off the ignition, turn to mum. She hasn't even registered that we've stopped. The memories battle away behind her eyes, her mouth works soundlessly.

The day is colder out than it looks from the warm interior of the car and as I tug my coat from the back seat I decide not to bother her with my plan. She wouldn't want to accompany me anyway.

Contrary as ever, she jumps and focuses when I open the car door. 'What's going on? Where are you going?'

The wrench from past to present is too abrupt, the sudden sweep of chill air on her skin too disorientating. She sounds afraid and I reach to soothe her. 'It's okay, mum, I'm just having a quick look at Granny Ivy's grave. I won't be long. You stay here in the warm.'

She fumbles out of the car and almost falls into the road. I have a quick sniff at her breath as I rush to steady her and she takes my arm.

'I'll come with you, love. Don't leave me here by myself.'

She leads the way through the side gate, into the graveyard. Waist deep amongst the markers for the dead, we both pause and squint across the fields, looking for our house. Her house. It's partially obscured by a tumbled, rusting barn that severs the landscape. Just the poke of a chimney and the thrusting oak are visible. The sea in the background, flat and grey.

'They're going to take that down.' Mum nods towards the barn. 'He died, the farmer. His family have sold the land off. They weren't interested in staying round here. This whole area will probably be an estate before too long.'

She doesn't sound too bothered but I'm enraged for her.

'That's awful. You don't want a housing estate right next to your back garden, surely? I'll give the council a ring.'

She scuffs her feet through the fallen leaves and starts to walk on. She looks as if she's floating through flaming tissue paper. 'Don't do it on my account, Fern. But do it for yourself if you want. The house will be yours, after all.'

She moves away and I let her go. We wander in different directions, pursuing our pieces of the past. Whenever I glance over she seems content to potter and mutter and so I leave her alone while I locate and tidy my grandparents' plot.

I run a hand gently over Granny Ivy's gravestone and use a fingertip to write 'beloved' before her name. The word imprints for a second on decades of decay before collapsing into the moss. The granite has acquired a gothic finish, coated as it is in bird droppings and draped with creeping weeds. It leans over my grandfather's grave as though the earth itself has shifted to allow a closer embrace. She would be pleased if she were here to see it.

I wander into the little side porch to look at the ivy carving on the window frame then stroll back to check on mum. She's picking her way through the overgrown grass at the far end of the graveyard and doesn't turn when I speak. 'What are you up to over here? I notice that you haven't bothered to do a damn thing to maintain Granny Ivy's final resting place. I bet you only pop over to sprinkle breadcrumbs over her crumbling bones and encourage the local bird life to crap on her …. Mum?'

She's got herself tangled up in brambles, thorny ropes cling around her ankles. She teeters and almost falls.

'Wait, mum, let me …' I bend to free her and swear as my fingers get scratched. Her legs are already laddered with blood. She stands patiently, staring over my head, humming something I can't quite catch.

'There you go. Take a big step now, and watch that clump by here.'

But she turns and walks away, wading further through the brambles. Every time it seems as if she's in danger of getting snarled up again she pushes through, hard, with her knees. I can hear small ripping sounds and hope very much that they are coming from her skirt and not her skin.

'Mum, for Christ's sake what are you doing? I'm not coming to get you if you fall over.'

She looks back at me and her face is soft with delight. The kind flush of the setting sun lends her a youthful beauty. She glances down, shuffles her feet to disturb the vegetation, and then stands still and swivels round, with a graceful roll of her hips that's almost a shimmy. The brambles swivel with her, lassoing her ankles. She doesn't notice.

'This is where I first met your father. Right here, in this spot. He was driving past and saw me dancing under this tree. He said he had to stop and speak to me, see if I was as lovely up close as I looked from a distance. And I was, back then.'

She starts to hum again and this time I can almost make out the tune. I wince at the sight of her torn legs and then shrug and lean back against a gravestone. There's antiseptic lotion in the house. 'I know you were, mum. I've seen the photos.'

I don't think she's heard me. She stands with her back straight and her head up as though waiting for someone. I follow her gaze to the gate and half expect to see the ghost of a man walk through it and towards us. Towards her. Gathering pace as he gets nearer, intent on nothing but her, on discovering her. I squint into the sun's afterglow and can almost see the urgent flicker of two shadows rushing to meet each other.

'When did he tell you that he was married?' I suddenly ask.

She jumps and frowns.

I ask it again, with real need. I want to know, had she been as cynical as him from the very start, as thoughtlessly determined to pursue her own pleasures, regardless of the consequences to herself, to his other family, or to me.

She sighs and wades back to me, for the first time noticing the state her legs are in. She lets out a yelp of horror at the dried smears of blood across her shins. I've punctured her mood and my punishment is that tight, closed look on her face. That resentful pout to her lips. But I'm determined not to drive her home, to her precious bottles, until she's answered my question. She needs to give me something. I need to know.

I tell her as much as I heave her out of the undergrowth and back onto the path. She pulls and hunches away, but then gives in and leans against me. Tired now, and eager to leave.

I ask again. We stop beside the car and she shivers, but I don't unlock it. 'Well? When did he tell you?'

She rubs her elbow as if it pains her and tugs at the door handle. Puts her free arm on the roof and rests her head on it. Her face is turned from me but I know that she's furious. 'Stop bullying me, Fern.'

I clench my hand around the keys until they dig into my palm. I don't look away. 'When did he tell you?'

She turns her head then and stares at me. There's a nerve flickering below her eye.

'Not for a while. I didn't even think … It was your bloody grandmother who guessed and told me to ask him. You can imagine how delighted she was. But we both decided to keep things as they were. He wouldn't leave his wife and I wouldn't leave him, so there didn't seem to be much choice but to keep things as they were.'

I poke the key roughly into the lock and turn it. Open the car door and hold it for her so that she can climb into the front seat. 'There's always choice, mum.'

She huddles into her coat as I start the engine and angle the hot air fan in her direction.

'How nice it must be to be you, Fern. How nice to lead such a pale life.'

I swing the car onto the road, past the heaped stone wall of the churchyard, and shudder when I see how centuries of sunlight striking the stones have bleached them of hue. They balance like infant's skulls, one on top of the other.

A Bird's Claw

Feathers speckled grey and white and beige across the grass. Feathers stained gaudy scarlet at their tips. And a frail, snapped leg, just the one, amongst the feast remains.

As you stooped to look I picked up the leg and lunged it, claw wagging on its broken stem, towards your face. It was just a joke, I was never going to touch you with it, but you made a disgusted noise and pushed my hand away, kept yours outstretched to create distance. You told me I was childish.

I wiped my palm on my dress and ran to catch you up but you refused to hold my hand, refused to even look at me. I tried to hug your arm and match my strides to yours, half-skipping to stay close, but our hips kept clashing and throwing me off rhythm. We lurched like that for a while, in silence.

You were angry with me. I thrilled with the newness of it. You were angry with me and I had the power to defuse or inflame this moment. How much damage would we do? How much would it hurt? More than saying goodbye? I let go of your arm and made a brittle, laughing comment about the difference in our ages. I think I called you an old man. You stopped and we faced each other, showed our teeth. We'd never done this before, didn't know how, but suddenly I wanted to, and so badly.

You started to speak and I mimicked your tone, repeated your words in a high, sing-song whine that pressed a nerve behind your eyes so that they grew wide and hard. You half turned away and I grabbed your arm and pulled you roughly back. I began to shout.

Do you remember what I said? Do you still think about it?

I can't recall anything but the exhilarating surge of spite and the need to take a word-axe to your roots and topple you. I hadn't realised I could be so cruel, hadn't realised how many layers of hurt had calcified beneath the crust of my smile. I stood and shouted.

Your lips drooped apart and I saw beyond the trembling pink your crooked bottom teeth. I couldn't breathe for tears.

You hugged me as I cried. You hushed my remorse. You told me that it didn't matter, that nothing had changed, that everything was going to be okay. And then you gave me your hand as we walked. It started to rain and you laughed and draped your jacket over me as we ran to the car.

After you'd gone I sat in my room and shivered as I tried to summon memory of what I might have said. I sat in the dark and whispered words I might have used. *Bastard. Dirty old man. Cheap kicks. Other woman. Whore.*

I couldn't remember a single thing. My mind had tipped itself upside down and emptied out all trace of our argument. There was nothing left but a sour taste along my gums. I brushed my teeth and rinsed my mouth, rubbed my tongue with soap until bubbles frothed iridescently around my gag, and by the next morning the sourness had gone.

4

I was fourteen when Granny Ivy's spirit shook itself loose from its nest below my rib cage during a nasty fever and flung itself onto the bedroom wall. Her final breath made solid and given physical shape.

Once the bout of coughing had subsided, I propped myself onto my elbow and watched as the thing I'd created scuttled and clung to the shadows. Rustling up to the ceiling and whispering, whispering words that I couldn't make out.

It was like a child's crayon drawing of a crow, all scrawled edges and funny lumps, but it looked at me with her eyes. I flung myself against my pillows and reached as high as I could, tearing at the air, scrabbling for it.

Come back to me.

When I think of that night I want to scoop up my fourteen-year-old self and hold her close; keep her safe from a world which my adult self knows doesn't allow for such whimsy. Yes, I was delirious, but I was also sure, am still sure, that my granny's soul was there, on my ceiling. And I couldn't bear to lose her twice.

My pillows reared up and pummelled me and I threw myself forward, onto my knees. The blankets twisted themselves around my wrists, pulling me down into the mattress. I rolled onto my back, legs pedalling the air, and spilled over the side of the bed, jarring my shoulder against the wardrobe. Its door swung slowly open and the mirror fastened to its dark-wood carcass distorted my face so that I loomed above myself like a stranger. I screamed for my mum.

She careered through the door a few seconds later, glass pitching in hand and ice cubes pirouetting across the room.

What? What's happened?

I could only thrash and gasp. She stared around her, above her, and then at me. Exasperation at the spillage of her precious drink sharpened her eyes and her voice.

For Christ's sake, what's wrong?

She slapped impatiently at the light switch.

The pillows now smooth and plump against the headboard. The blankets layered in neat squares. The creature had retreated.

I climbed back into bed, hot and tearful, trying to speak, and then another coughing fit overcame me. I was desperate for one of mum's ice cubes.

With rare maternal understanding she scooped one up from the rug and blew on it to dislodge the fluff, then ran it across my temples until I was quiet again. She was so gentle.

It's okay now. You're running a fever. Seeing things that aren't there. It's okay now.

She stayed with me while she finished her drink, patting my hand between sips, and then she went back downstairs for a refill, but she left the light on.

It took another couple of days for the fever to subside and another week before I could trust my legs enough to bear my weight. I lay and stared at the ceiling and read *The Shining* between naps. I thought about the thing I'd seen.

I wondered what it had been trying to say. I worried that it had been something important. I worried that it missed me.

My bedside light scorched holes through the night for months afterwards, scalding the shadows so that they leapt and tumbled across my walls. My reflection hesitated just beyond the lamp's glow, flickered just out of reach, but I was too scared to look in case I didn't recognise myself.

I'd carried Granny Ivy's soul around inside me for over a year, had swallowed it with her dying breath and kept it locked up next to my own. I'd imagined them bumping gently together when I walked, like twins in a womb. Through colds and stomach upsets I'd held on, and now one bad fever had rattled it loose and sent it crashing into the wall.

So I started to skip meals, saving room inside me in case it came back. Especially now that I knew how big it was.

I began to barter my way through the days. If I got from the chemistry lab to the art room in exactly seventy steps, it would return to me. If I held my breath on the school bus, from the park to the bicycle shop, it would return. If I could stay awake all night. If I could …

I developed a phobia about spiders and then was unable to sit still in class. The sudden swoop of a bird in the yard had me calling out, running for the exit with my arms outstretched. Opening my mouth wide, stretching my lips apart with my fingers until they cracked and tore. Searching out the ink-scrawl shifting across the sky's slate and willing it to return to me.

The skewed logic of those months, the logic that comes screaming out of loss and hope, makes sense to me even now. Am I really a more fulfilled person, less lonely, without the rituals I'd once framed my world with? Like mum with her gin, and Granny Ivy with her magic, I needed them. But I should have been more discreet.

Those few friends who hadn't yet been put off by mum's habit of flinging up her skirts and dancing drunkenly around the house with her knickers on show began to slink away from me, as if strangeness could be contagious. Playground whispers soon became a hum that reached even the ears of the teachers and I was sent to the school nurse. She stripped me of my uniform and turned me this way and that with hands so cold they made my skin wince and pucker. She spoke over my head to her colleague as if I were deaf, or absent.

You've heard about her mother? The apple doesn't fall far from the tree.

I didn't understand the reference but the image made me think of mum, cheeks Gala flushed, dancing under the oak.

Once nothing was found to be physically wrong with me it was decided that I was experiencing some kind of emotional disturbance and mum was called in to speak to the form mistress. That was the last thing either of us wanted. She ignored the first three summonses, chose instead to shut herself into the living room on the day in question, curtains closed and radio on. She was usually drunk, and sometimes asleep, when I returned from school with another note. I'd slip it into her fist and then go to put the kettle on, returning with a mug of strong, bitter coffee. The note would have disappeared by then, magicked away as if it had never been, and she wouldn't look at me as she raised herself into a sitting position and tucked her trembling hands out of sight.

I knew how scared she was, for both of us, but I never said anything. Some cold, stubborn part of me was curious to see what would happen if all this were allowed to carry on for much longer. My present was pursuing her past and I'd soon be catching it up. Racing it to the place where pretty dresses weren't allowed. A part of me even wanted to go to that place, and make **her** wait at home for the postcard that never arrived. See how she liked it.

It never came to that.

I can still remember parts of that conversation with my teacher, as I listened from my seat in the hall.

Miss Gilbert, it's good to finally meet you … Fern's a very capable pupil, one of the brightest in her form … She seems to be suffering from some kind of neurotic hysteria …

My mum's voice shrill with panic, vowels pulsing like a blackbird's alarm call. They snipped through the door's wood as if it were paper, skidded along the polished floorboards and into all the classrooms. I sat with my head in my hands and tried not to hear the straining silence of my classmates, the odd, embarrassed giggle.

She started her period last year. That's probably what brought this on. All those hormones swilling around.

I nearly ran then, but where would I have gone? It wasn't as if I had an indulgent aunt waiting to take me in and feed me biscuits. I'd carelessly lost Granny Ivy's spirit, and I'd chased my own father off. It was just me and mum now.

So I remained where I was and started to count the cracks in the ceiling tiles. If each tile had an even number of cracks, it would return ....

It was when the talk turned to possible solutions, possible therapeutic interventions, that mum's voice really took off. I didn't have to see her to know that she was clutching at herself, scrabbling at the skin of her arms with those ragged fingernails. The expression of cool disdain on the face across the desk from her, the dignified contempt. So at odds with my mum's throbbing, twitching attempts at control.

Would you like a glass of water, Miss Gilbert? You seem agitated.

A big glass of something stronger was what she'd like. What she needed. She cleared her throat and shifted, constantly shifted, on her chair. I held my breath and cradled my kneecaps, and started to count the cracks on the floor tiles.

But then something happened that surprised me. My mum straightened her back and met the form mistress' eyes, and she curled her lip. I could **hear** her doing this.

No, thank you, Mrs Mitchell, I'm quite all right. I'm so grateful to you for your interest in Fern but there's no need for you to involve anyone else at this stage. I'll talk to her tonight. No, please don't get up.

Her voice was sweet and low, with just a hint of sharpness; a lemon segment rolled in brown sugar and brushed across the lips. A chair squealed as it was pushed along the floor and then the door opened and she stood there before me. She pulled on her faded satin gloves and nodded a goodbye without turning her head, glided from the room as steadily as if she were the figurehead on the prow of a ship. I stood up and followed in her wake, without speaking.

As we both reached the double doors at the end of the corridor, where the outside world gleamed distortedly through reinforced glass, she paused and blinked at me. She looked bewildered.

Haven't you got lessons to go to?

I shrugged and linked my arm through hers, planted my shoulder against the thick wood, preparing to push. I smiled at her.

Double gym. Don't worry, you wrote me a note excusing me for the rest of term. Let's go home.

She hesitated and I thought that she was going to withdraw her arm, send me off to join my classmates, but then she smiled back and squeezed my flesh.

Sod it, let's stop on the way for an ice cream, shall we?

She led us out of the building, into an afternoon fondant-sweet and drowsy with cherry blossom. I loved her then more than I ever had before, and when a crow swooped low over my head I didn't falter or look up. Her warm arm against mine was all the comfort I needed.

*

While mum's in the bathroom I sneak into her bedroom and have a good snoop around. The curtains are drawn against the morning and I pull them wide and open the window to let in some air. They are the curtains of my childhood, the graceful pink dancers, now hanging limp and unkempt as discarded mistresses.

I finger the straggly hems, the threads trailing like un-brushed hair. Beyond them, silvered by dew, the oak tree strains to grasp at the fabric. It's so close to the house now that if I lean over the sill and reach my arm out I can touch one of the furthest flung branches. I lean and reach, twist off a leaf. The oak will soon be completely naked, etched like a filigree brooch against yet another winter sky. I wonder whether it's aware of my presence, my touch. Whether it resents me robbing it of one more leaf, when it's already lost so many.

Water rushes into the pipes and I turn my attention to the bedside cabinet, rifling quickly through the little cupboard. I check the dressing table, the chest of drawers, under the bed.

The jewellery box that she inherited from Granny Ivy gapes on the rocking chair, half buried by clothes and spilling a rainbow tangle across the dark wood. I dig around inside it, scooping out huge chunks of costume jewels. A pretty little amethyst ring catches my eye and I slip it into my pocket. It'll be mine eventually anyway. My fingernails catch on paper at the base of the box. A photograph.

I prise it out and take it over to the window. It's a faded black and white one of my father and me, worn shiny and thin. He's turned away from the camera, in the act of swinging me onto the bonnet of his car, and I'm slightly blurred as I sail through the air, legs stuck out rigidly in front of me. I'm squealing or laughing and there's a field in the frame behind the car. I wonder if this photo was taken just before the infamous hand-biting scene. But I look too happy, as if I'm having too much fun, to be moments away from sinking my teeth into his flesh. I bow close over the tiny image of myself and examine it but there's definitely no hint of a snarl on that cheery little face, no matter which way I turn the picture.

I pile the gems back into Granny Ivy's jewellery box and grab at the heap of clothes. There, hidden beneath her dressing gown, I finally find mum's cache of tablets. The familiar striped boxes of anti-depressants and sleeping pills. Others with complicated names which I don't recognise. These are unopened, the security seals pristine. I empty the lot onto the floor and stir through it with my foot.

The bathroom door opens and I hear mum shuffle down the hall. She jumps when she sees me and lets out a small shriek. Then she spots the spill of cardboard on the rug and her face becomes smooth and shuttered, impenetrable. 'What are you doing with those?'

I pick up one of the boxes and read out the name of the drug. 'What are these ones for, mum? And why haven't you been taking them?' I don't let her answer. 'They're for your heart, aren't they?'

She sits on the edge of the bed and starts a one-handed shuffle into her socks, wincing. 'I could really do with a hand here, Fern.'

I kneel at her feet and we work together, silently, to get her dressed. She's seemingly engrossed in the task and studiously avoids looking at me. The helpless way she sticks her legs out for me to slide her trousers on disarms my anger and I'm still groping to recapture it when the phone begins its shrill wail beneath us. She turns to me eagerly. 'Aren't you going to get that? It could be the restaurant, or Rick.'

'It's not a restaurant, mum, it's a cafe. And I'm not managing it, I just waitress there, as I keep telling you. They have no reason to call.' I stand up and lean over her. 'I want to know why you're not taking your pills.'

'It's none of your business, I've already told you that.' She tries to get up but I don't step away and she butts me gently in the chest before losing her balance and sinking back onto the bed. She rubs her head and glares up at me. 'I could report you to Social Services.'

I laugh and, after a moment, she joins in. But the scowl is still there.

'Is this why you want me to look for dad all of a sudden? Because you're ill and you're not going to take your tablets or even stop drinking? A kind of slow motion suicide. How can you be so selfish?'

She takes advantage of a weakness in my stance to heave herself up and push past me. There's no pretence at humour now, from either of us.

'You're a fine one to talk about being selfish. How long has it been since you visited me? If Tommy hadn't phoned you wouldn't be here at all and we both know it. I don't want to take the tablets so I'm not going to and you can't make me. I don't want to stop drinking either. It's all I've got. As to your father, there's no suddenly about it. I want to know why he left and I want him back. I've always wanted that.'

I hold my hands up. 'You're right, I can't make you.' I bend to pick up the boxes. 'I might as well bin them then, if you're sure.'

She stares at me, at the tablets, and then turns to pull the window closed. 'Yes. You might as well. And then you can get on with looking for Lawrence. Do something useful while you're here.'

'Then where do you suggest I start? You've already said you don't have anything I can use to trace him. I'm not a bloody magician.'

Mum grimaces quickly over at her bookcase, a brief tic of guilt. The bookcase is slippery with magazines and I decide to give her a gin with her lunch and go through every one of them while she has her afternoon nap.

'Well, I'm sure you'll think of something,' she says.

It's nearly lunchtime when I get back from watching the late morning ferry come into dock. Mum's sat in the front room, chair angled towards the window and body tense with watchfulness. I can see her face creased into corrugations of hope and anxiety as I open the gate and walk up the path, and I wince and wave apologetically. 'Only me.'

She bites her lip and leans back, sinks below the ripples of the half-net. I have a sudden image of her dead in her chair, drowned and serene. She's sulking but I reckon my peace offering, the most expensive bottle of gin the local supermarket has to offer, will raise a smile, or at the very least a grudging word of thanks.

I get both. And she doesn't even notice the tablet I've crushed into her food, so busy is she sucking down that second drink before I change my mind. She's half asleep before I've finished washing up and she doesn't complain when I tuck a blanket around her and pull the curtains closed. I stand still in the centre of the room for a moment, enjoying the dusky drape of semi-darkness in the middle of the day and the accompanying thrill of the illicit. She's snoring before I've reached the top of the stairs.

Every shelf of her bookcase is packed with bridal magazines. Too many to count. I can follow the trends of decades as I leaf through them, shake them upside down over the rug and then put them aside. Hazy young women, frothy with lace, gasp and clasp their hands in delight at this fulfilment of their life's dream. The pages are brittle from years of licked thumbs. Scraps of paper mark certain articles. I imagine mum sitting patiently through years of perms and trims, empty carrier bag folded in her pocket, the petty thief's flush on her cheeks. And then hurrying home with her latest acquisitions and poring over them for hours, studying the section on wedding etiquette and deliberating between a veil and a head dress.

Tucked into one of the pages, covering a dress that must surely have been The Dress for mum, is part of what looks like a spell, scribbled onto a sheet of creamy writing paper. A love spell? My mother's writing but definitely my grandmother's words.

... Take in your cupped palms two flaming pieces of fire opal and two gentling pieces of rose quartz. Linger a while with sweet thoughts ...

Had she written it from memory? From years of stolen peeks at her mother's *Cooking Book*? I wondered if she'd ever cast the spell. It clearly hadn't worked, if she did.

On the bottom shelf of the bookcase, buried beneath the last pile of euphoric smiles, I see an envelope, stiff with photographs. Photographs of my father.

My father walking away from the camera, towards our gate, with me in his arms.

My father asleep in a bed, in a room I don't recognise.

My father leaning over me in a wood, one huge hand engulfing each of mine.

My father sitting behind the wheel of his car, staring down at a map.

My father cradling a sleeping me to his chest, a book propped open on my back.

My father naked, towelling himself down, framed in an open doorway.

My father...

I sit and look through them, again, and again, and again. There must be ten or more and in none of them is he looking at the camera or holding himself with the self-conscious poise of the observed.

I run downstairs and throw them at mum, scattering him over her. 'Look at these. So much for having nothing. What else are you hiding?'

She jerks awake and holds her hands up to her eyes, blinks down at the photographs, up at me. Down again. 'How did you find these? Have you been going through my room?'

I'm too angry to feel any embarrassment, too shocked by the images of my father, naked, vulnerable, captured and committed to paper without his knowledge.

'I knew you were lying to me, hiding things. Look at him. He didn't have a clue that you were taking his picture. Do you know how weird that is? Like you're his stalker rather than his lover; the mother of his child. No wonder he left.'

She starts to gather the photographs up and push them into

the pocket of her cardigan. She won't look at me now. Her movements are hesitant and graceless.

'Don't say things like that, Fern, don't be cruel. These are private. They're mine.'

I bend to pick one up which had spun to the floor unnoticed. It's another picture of my father and me together, my toddler-self walking, penguin-like, on his feet. We're laughing.

I sit down on the rug and stare at it. 'Look at him, mum. He's laughing. He's having fun. With me. He looks like a proper dad. He looks like he loves me.'

She stays silent. I try to retrieve my anger. 'Anyway, you can't decide what's important and what isn't. There could have been something in one of these that could help. What else are you hiding?'

Mum holds her hand out for the photograph and when I lay it onto her palm she smiles down at it, stroking it gently with her forefinger. She still won't look at me.

'Maybe you should tell me what you've been hiding, Fern.'

I draw my knees up to my chest and wrap my arms around myself, holding my heart close. 'What are you talking about?'

She looks up then, leans slowly over so that our foreheads are nearly touching. 'I know you're pregnant.'

I shake my head and start to say something, some kind of denial, but the words keep slipping out of my head. She waits while I gather myself, clear my throat. 'How? How did you …?'

She shrugs and looks defiant, a little sheepish. 'You're not the only snoop in the family. I saw the picture of the scan in your handbag. I've been waiting for you to tell me, but then I finally realised that you weren't going to. Were you?'

I don't answer her.

'Is it Rick's?' Mum asks. 'Have you told him? Is he pleased? You know it'll be a girl, don't you? You know it will be.'

I stand up and walk to the door.

'Then god help the poor little bugger.'

A Blood Soaked Shoe Lace

You said it was your fault for walking too quickly, for making me rush in my heels to keep up. I never told you that I was frowning down at my snagged black nylons, at the pearl-glint of flesh zigzagging down the thigh. They were new on that evening as well.

The broken bottle bit deep into my shin as I spilled onto the ground. The tiny crunching noise it made as it broke the skin was somehow satisfying and I didn't scream until I saw the glossy jut of glass below my knee and my blood on the cobbles.

You'd been speaking, throwing words over your shoulder as you strode ahead, and then you were by my side and silent as you stared. I scrabbled for you but you held me away and raised my leg, braced my foot against your chest. You pushed me gently back so that I could see the apricot smear of street lamps tainting the night and you told me to be still.

I thought I knew what you were doing and even despite the pain and the panic I wouldn't have stopped you, would even have welcomed your body on mine, but you unlaced your shoe and tied the brown cord around my ankle. Tight, and then tighter. You lowered my leg to the ground and raised me up and the blood poured. I screamed again. And then I was in your arms and you were running to the car. A stray tomcat, tatty as an over-loved teddy bear, balanced on a dustbin lid and kept sombre watch as you wrapped your suit jacket around my leg. Its faded eyes fixed on me and I couldn't look away.

At the hospital they stitched me and scolded you for tying the tourniquet below the wound. You held my hand and told me you were sorry. By the time they finally let us go we'd missed the film so we went straight to the hotel with our champagne in your weekend bag and me, a hop-a-long, beside you. I didn't really need to limp, the painkillers had done their job, but I liked the way you slowed your pace and held my waist.

The bath was too hot but I got in anyway, leg straddling the side as you stroked water over me with a flannel. Foam in scented peaks around my face. You kissed each toe and wrapped me in a towel, carried me to the bed. The lamps were lit and I lay and watched you undress. Watched you tremble. When I stretched out my arms to gather you close you shook your head and sat on the edge of the bed, face in hands.

So much blood.

I curled my body behind yours and licked the abacus parade of bone at the nape of your neck. I didn't speak.

I'm going to take better care of you, Iris, I promise.

We were quiet for a while. Your flesh flickered and dampened beneath my tongue. Your breath came fast. I knew you'd turn around.

Later, in your sleep, you muttered my name and clasped my hip so tightly I nearly cried out. The imprint of your fingers stayed on my skin long after you'd dropped me home and left me once again.

5

I was sixteen when I fell in love with the guitarist of the school's rock band. I was sixteen when I got pregnant.

He was sat outside the science lab, guitar across his lap and notepad on his knee. As I walked past he began to pluck at the strings of the instrument, humming a tune. I knew he was watching me. I fumbled with the straps of my book bag, slowing my pace until I was stood before him, and then I dropped the bag and began to dance. We stared at each other as I stepped back and forth, swinging my hips to his song, and then he jumped up and came over to me, wrapped his large palms around my upper arms and pulled me against him. His dark hair pooled against my cheek, tickling the corner of my mouth. It smelt of Love Hearts. I shuddered and leaned into him, and finally understood what kept my mother waiting at the living room window day after day.

He knew my reputation; the crow chasing and the compulsive counting. He wrote anguished poetry in clumsy, stumbling rhyme that tortured the ear (*'I gasped and flailed / under the stab of your eyes / You laughed as I swayed / You told nothing but lies.'*) and he was looking for a muse. He'd been born on the mainland and his otherness set him apart from the other boys, the islanders.

By the end of that day I'd skipped my first maths, English literature and geography classes, and I'd stolen my first bottle of wine from the off-licence near the park, the one that my mum never went into. By the end of that day I knew how it felt to slot my naked hipbones against another person's. The gentle scuff and scattered goosebumps as delighted skin crept across delighted skin, and then the hard press of the skeleton beneath.

Again! And again! And again!

Two bodies curling up and stretching out and winding around each other. Two bodies grasping and clutching and cradling. He was the oak tree that guarded my home, and I the honeysuckle that clung and gripped, that scaled his body until he was completely covered by me.

His parents worked and so he had a key and the house to himself for a couple of hours each day after school. After we'd tugged our clothes back on and opened the windows to release the moist tang of each other, he'd read me his poetry or sing one of his songs and I'd listen and smile, watching his mouth, shivering with the need to feel his weight upon me again. He begged me to stay on past six, to meet his mum and dad, but I always refused. I didn't want to see him as somebody's son, as existing apart from me and away from me. Just sixteen, and I was already an echo of my mother, carving out a private world for me and my love, working to separate it, and him, from the realities of meal times and laundry and all those other domestic routines. And besides, I'd then have to return the favour and there was no way I was going to let him anywhere near my shabby home or my mother's gin-soaked breath.

I was fascinated by his house, by its tidiness and its lemon-zest smell. I looked through the cupboards while he dozed and discovered furniture polish and special cleaners to apply to metal and leather. I'd collect the brass ornaments that were crowded on the mantelpiece and spread them out across the dining room table, anointing and buffing them until they gleamed, and then carefully replacing them. I wonder if anyone ever noticed. I sprayed my shoes with the polish every day so that I'd take some of that clean smell home with me, and there I'd walk from room to room, stomping my feet, and imagine it drifting off onto the carpets and rugs.

The refrigerator was filled with food that I had never tasted: avocados and olives and soft French cheeses. I sampled each new flavour, my fingertips leaving crescent-shaped grooves in the Camembert. In the bedrooms I would tread carefully between bed and dressing table, wary of the beige carpets so soft my footprints left dents. The bedside drawers were a treasure trove of old diaries and exotic looking ointments, tins with tiny teeth inside and little pots of hand creams. My mum's bedside drawer never held anything more exciting than a bottle of gin and her sleeping pills.

Photographs in silver frames marched up the walls of the staircase and clustered on the half-landing. Faces, smiling or solemn, gazed at me and at each other. Arms grasped shoulders and hands clasped waists. Mother and father, mother and son, father and son. This unabashed flaunting of the bonds of love and family made me feel queasy and hollow, but nevertheless compelled me to return to stare again and again.

I took one of the photographs home, a group one of the whole family together, grandparents as bookends, all sitting in a line on a beach and juggling ice creams and sun hats. My poet, grinning and gritty with sand, teetering on toddler legs, held up a dead crab triumphantly. I eased it from its hook and pulled the hook from the wall, licking my finger to smooth out the puncture hole left behind. Once home, I wrapped the photo in a pillowcase and slid it into the oak tree: the keeper of my secrets since I was old enough to have any. I nestled the bundle into the head-height cavity carved between two branches, imagining it settling deep inside that wooden heart, flavouring the sap and gilding the leaves. My oak, now a literal family tree.

I saw my love one weekend, in the newsagents with his mother, and I watched them together for a while before he turned and spotted me. The rage I felt then, the grief, left me breathless and tearful. In those moments before he registered my presence he belonged utterly to her. It was as if I didn't exist. Was he thinking about me? When she picked up a music magazine and tapped him on the wrist, and he glanced down at it, shook his head and plucked it from her hands, was he calculating the hours until he could see me again? He didn't look as if he was. He didn't even look like him. Boredom and embarrassment at being out with his mum had hardened the angles of his beautiful boy's face and his eyes flicked constantly from place to place. When he laughed it was grudgingly, unwillingly.

I'd been in the chemist's for the last hour, glazing myself with different scents until my head ached and I smelt like a bowl of potpourri. I wanted to march up to them and reclaim him, make him mine again, but I also wanted to run away and change my clothes, shower and brush my hair, and then return as clean and untainted as their home. I stood and stared.

And then he turned his head and saw me. He jumped as if I'd reached over and prodded him, but then he smiled and started to walk towards where I was huddled by the comics. He said something to his mother and she looked straight at me, her face creased with pleasure. She followed after him and they reached me together, standing shoulder to shoulder, closer to each other than to me. My poet said my name, said hers, and she smiled and offered a laughing comment, her hand on his arm and then on the nape of his neck. They were the same height.

I don't remember what I said, or if I said anything at all. I couldn't take my eyes from her hand as it moved against the skin of his neck, cupping the knob of bone at the top of his spine. He grimaced and wriggled, bringing his shoulders up to his ears, and shrugged the hand away. There was an expectant silence.

She was dressed in a pretty cream skirt and blouse, this mother, and her hair was the same dark colour as his. Her eyes were different, though, lighter and wider, or maybe they just looked that way because of her use of shadow and mascara. Her fingernails were painted coral.

Fern?

My poet finally moved to touch me but she moved at the same time, her face a frown of concern.

Are you okay, honey?

And they touched me together, bumping hands against my arm.

I recoiled, pushed past them both, harder than I'd intended, and she stumbled backwards. I didn't pause to see if she was all right. I barely made it to the door of the shop before I threw up.

They drove me home and I sobbed for the entire journey, doubled over with my face in my lap. The boy sat with me in the back of the car, his skin waxy with nausea and distaste. He patted me awkwardly, hissed his helplessness to his mother. He was terrified of my tears.

The mother was terrified of something else. She stopped the car in the lane outside our house and helped me out, held onto me for a moment.

Is this the only time you've been sick lately, sweetheart?

I could make out the outline of mum at the living room window, lamp-lit, haloed in bronze. As I gently pulled away and started to walk towards the front door, the outline wavered and melted. This wasn't the car she was expecting, but what joy must she have felt, just for a second, when it actually stopped outside the house? Enough joy to salve the last decade and more?

As I walked up to the front door I realised that I had become my mother. But unlike my mother, I was going to learn my lesson, and I was going to learn it right now. We both loved too fiercely, and too much, but unlike her I wouldn't ever again wrench at my heart with both hands and thrust it with such wanton eagerness at another person. I wouldn't ever again scour myself out with love, until I was raw and emptied of me, ready to be filled by them.

That's the great thing about being sixteen, isn't it? You really do believe that you can unhook yourself cleanly from a future dictated by blood and conditioning, simply because you want to, because you've decided to. I even had the audacity to pity my mother a little, for her helplessness in love and her lack of strength. So different from me, I thought. In the years since then, of course, I've been too busy repeating all of her patterns to have time for pity, for either of us.

I lay in bed that night with my hands laid across my stomach, kneading at the tiny soul that squirmed and somersaulted beneath my palms. Tomorrow I would go to the doctor and ask him to help me destroy it. The next morning the cramps hit, and by the next night I had nothing left to show for my first love affair apart from bloodied bed sheets, a taste for olives, and a silver-framed photograph of strangers buried in a tree.

*

The standoff lasts for three days. I tend to mum's needs with exaggerated care, checking and double-checking that she's got enough cushions behind her back, or preparing meals from Granny Ivy's old recipe books that neither of us enjoy. For her part, mum winces and gasps theatrically whenever I lift anything heavier than a mug and tries to lever herself from her chair every evening to take her own plate into the kitchen.

'I can do it, love. You just sit there and rest for a bit.'

She's determined that my pregnancy should trump her dodgy heart and I have to reluctantly concede that she's scoring more points in our little competition. She's clearly a pro. Neither of us has mentioned the argument that brought us to this and I'm guessing she feels as righteous and wronged as I do about the snooping accusations.

I finally snap on the third evening when she follows me into the kitchen, intent on warming me a mug of milk ('You need the calcium, lovey') whilst I'm just as intent on mixing her a weak gin and tonic to wash down her bedtime painkiller. We use our hips as weapons as we jostle next to the fridge, both scrabbling to get the door open. I don't want to knock her bad arm around too much but she's not hampered by such qualms. Her nails are longer than mine and she doesn't baulk at employing them to her advantage.

I snatch the milk bottle from her and slam it onto the sideboard. 'For god's sake. Will you just go and sit down and leave me to do this? I can manage basic tasks.'

She smiles at me sympathetically and wipes at the spilled milk with a piece of kitchen towel. 'Hormones?'

I open my mouth to scream and she pats me on the arm, shuffles quickly out. When I join her a few minutes later she's gracious in victory, accepting her glass with a word of thanks and marginal smirk. I want to kill her. We sit in silence and I strain to think of some way to redress the balance.

'Where's that bloody old woman gone now?' she asks. She frowns down at her feet, wiggles her toes. 'What if he comes and I need to go out? I can't leave you alone.'

I forget my scheming. 'What bloody old woman?'

She shrugs and is sullen. 'You know exactly who I mean.'

I watch her for a moment. 'Are you talking about Granny Ivy?'

She ignores me. Her toes tap and roll constantly inside her slippers, her face is a twist of concentration.

'Mum?'

And then she jerks and covers her face as the present reasserts itself. I move to hug her but she clears her throat and then thrusts her empty glass at me. 'I want to go to bed now.' She heaves herself up, stumbling slightly as she turns to leave the room.

I can't resist the malicious impulse to rush forward with pronounced concern and help her, seize her around the shoulders and walk her towards the door. 'There we go, mum, one step at a time. That's the way.'

She doesn't even seem to notice my presence, let alone bridle at my tone. The competition has clearly ended and I feel cheated that she was the one to score the last direct hit. I steer her towards the stairs and then stand back and watch when she shrugs me away bad-temperedly. 'Bugger off, Fern. I can get myself to bed, you know, I'm not completely helpless.'

From my vantage point in the very centre of the car park I can see the full sweep of the dock below me. I get out of the car and walk past the clutter of picnic benches, swinging my binoculars. Just in time to hop over the barrier and settle myself onto the heather. I'm alone up here today, pressed between the sulky violet of the sky and the fidgeting grey of the sea. The approaching storm is vivid against the horizon, the distant loom of Sorel no more than a bruise in the mist.

Through my binoculars the last mainland ferry of the afternoon carves its way towards the safety of Spur's harbour. It races the billowing clouds, occasionally tangles in them before tearing itself loose and surging on. There's no one on deck.

Below me the taxis are lined up along the dock, hopeful of their fares. I try to locate Tommy and think I recognise the back of his head when he turns and stretches. Yes, it's definitely him. I watch for a while as he chats to the other drivers and smokes a cigarette, until a blast from the ferry's horn distracts us both.

There aren't many passengers for this crossing and I reckon there'll be even less for the evening one. The sea is starting to fling itself against the harbour wall in great, angry fistfuls, arcing spray over the cobbles. I stay where I am, hunched amongst the heather and above it all, dry for the moment, until the last car and the last foot passenger have reeled onto solid ground, and then I lower the binoculars and get up.

Tommy beeps into the car park and stops alongside me. 'I thought it was you, love. You're going to get yourself a reputation, lurking up here every day. What are you watching for?'

I lean in through the window to hug him. 'Hopefully more *French Lieutenant's Woman* than *Play Misty For Me*. I have a cloak if you think the distinction should be clarified.'

He laughs and gets out of the car. 'How are things going with your mum? Did she get the potatoes I left on the step the other day?'

'Yes, and she said to thank you if I saw you before she did.' I hesitate for a moment, torn between wanting to confide in him but also keep my mother's secrets. The desire to shift a little of the burden wins out. He'll still be here when I've gone, after all, and she'll need someone to keep an eye on her.

He nods when I tell him about her heart. 'It doesn't surprise me, Fern. And if that's her choice, to let it take her without a fight, there's nothing we can do.'

I decide not to say anything about crushing up the tablets and putting them in her food.

'But don't you think she's being selfish?' I ask. 'To just lie back and accept something she can change if she wants to? I suppose that's the way she's always been, though. Why choose life, and happiness, if you can lock the world out and do a Miss Havisham instead? So much more glamorous. So much easier.' I want him to feel some outrage, or at the very least fake a little, for me.

He shakes his head at me. 'Don't sneer at her, love.' And I'm immediately chastened. We start to walk to my car.

'I found some photographs of my father a few days ago,' I say. 'She'd hidden them away. Some were of him and me together and we both looked really happy. I'd forgotten that, that there was ever anything good between us.' I glance at him. 'It made me feel sad, but in a nice way. It made me realise how much I want to find him, or at least find out what happened to him and why he left. I've spent most of my life denying that I ever had a father, or taking the blame for him going. Now I want to hear *him* tell me it was my fault. I think I want to hear him tell me it wasn't.'

Tommy takes my keys from my hand and opens the car door for me. I wait for him to say something in response but he lights a cigarette and looks up at the sky, holding his palm out as if he fears rain. I touch his arm. 'Tommy?'

'I've got to go, love, there might be customers waiting in town. You should get back to your mum.'

I get into the car like an obedient child, but then swing round and plant my feet back on the ground so that he can't shut the door. 'I thought you could help me. I know it's probably the last thing you want to do but mum's not letting on that she remembers anything at all. You were always driving around the island in your taxi, though, so maybe you saw where he went when he left her. And you were so close to Granny Ivy, you must have talked about him.'

He drops his cigarette and stamps on it. 'I don't want to get involved, Fern, it's not my business.'

'But if you know anything…'

He turns away and flicks a hand out in farewell. 'You give your mum my best, and I'll be round to see you both soon.'

I don't shut the car door until he drives out of the car park.

It starts to rain and I hope he can see me in his rear view mirror, getting wet, waiting for him to turn round.

Mum's in a foul temper when I get home. I don't think she's moved from her chair at all in the last couple of hours since I've been out.

'Where have you been?' she hisses as I lean past her to close the window. 'Fat lot of help you are, disappearing off for hours and leaving me sat here in a draft all by myself. I don't know why you bothered to come home at all. What if I'd needed a drink?'

I kiss her on the cheek. 'Stop your whining, you old bag, and I'll get you a drink now. Orange juice?'

She jerks her head away and glares at me. 'What do you think?'

I look at my watch. 'I think you can wait another hour or two for anything stronger than that.'

She reaches for the tv remote and I wink at her and leave the room before she can throw it at me.

The glass of juice, decorated with a paper umbrella and straw, doesn't conjure up a smile. Mum refuses to even unfold her arms to take it so I slide it onto the coffee table by her side and take a seat opposite her.

'I saw Tommy today, when I was out,' I tell her. 'He said he'll be round soon to visit.'

Mum doesn't look up. I dip forward in my chair and prod her quickly on her good arm. 'Oh, come on, cheer up.'

She lets out a squawk and folds her upper body around her sling, rocking backwards and forwards. 'You just hit me. I can't believe you just did that.' She cowers away and clutches at her blanket when I shift towards her. 'Don't touch me.'

'Oh, for fuck's sake.' I settle back and reach for my own

drink. 'Shall I get you a gin? Is that going to put you in a better mood?'

I can see the hesitation, the brief calculation, but her spite is greater than her thirst right now. She stops rocking and looks straight at me. 'Don't you dare use that word at me. I think you should go. You've been here long enough.'

We sit for a while in silence and I follow the swirls and patterns of the rug with my eye, noting the patches where the wool has thinned, and the colours dimmed. Those patches where decades of heels and toes have trod and rubbed and laid tiny bits of themselves down. My grandparents, my parents, myself, we're all there in the weave of the fabric, layered one on top of the other. Soon my child will be added to the jumble, and maybe, in time, my grandchild.

I clear my throat so that my voice won't break or falter. 'You can't send me away. You'll never be able to cope without me. You'll drink from the moment you get up until the moment you go to bed.'

She snorts at that. 'I only drink as fast as you pour. And how do you think I've managed for these years, when you took off and didn't look back? I've been just fine, Fern. I'm still here aren't I? I don't need you.'

As if to emphasise her point she hoists herself out of her chair and bends to pick up her glass. She sways as she straightens, but we both pretend not to notice. I hear her shuffle around the kitchen, opening and closing cupboard doors. She won't be able to reach the gin but I know she won't ask for help now. I stay in the front room and listen out in case she attempts to climb on a chair, but she obviously decides not to risk her dignity and returns with the glass still full of juice.

I try to take her hand when she sits back down. 'But what

about looking for dad? I thought you wanted that more than anything. If you make me leave now then you'll never get to see him again. You'll never know why he left.'

She shrugs. 'I've changed my mind about looking for him. Leave the past in the past. And I already know why he left, don't I?' The look she gives me makes my fingers itch to give her another prod, and on the bad arm this time.

'Well, tough,' I tell her, 'I'm staying and I'm looking for him, just like I promised. Because the past isn't just the past for you, is it? It's your present and your future, and it's time that all stopped. If you want me to leave then try and make me, I'm not budging. I'm going to look for him and I'm going to find him, and there's nothing you can do about it.'

I stand up, wait for her to respond, then walk over to switch the television on. 'I'm going to make dinner now. You stay in here and have a good sulk. Yell out if you need anything.'

'You always were a contrary little bitch,' she shouts as I leave the room.

A Dried Fern Leaf

You tried to be a father to her but she took against you from the moment she was first placed in your arms. She won't remember the wooden toys you bought her, or the furtive kisses dropped onto her neck. The way you looked at her; that ferocious love that used to be just for me.

But she'd scream and kick, rigid with fury against your chest, her tiny body convulsed with contempt. And you'd panic and pass her back and I'd settle her immediately. Limp against my shoulder and then asleep in her basket with her thumb in her mouth. And it would be just the two of us again. Me and you. For a short time, until she needed a feed or a change, it was like she never was.

Only, things weren't the same. Even after my swollen body deflated and my breasts sprang back to tautness, ready to be reclaimed by you, I smelt more like her than like myself. Talcum powder and the sour tang of milk drying on skin. No amount of scrubbing or scent would take that away.

Do I seem resentful? I'm not actually. Not anymore. I did blame her for you leaving. I *do* blame her. But I'm not bitter, not now. I fought with you, with my mother, and with my own fear, to keep her. Nobody wanted her. And then she tunnelled her way into the world, splitting me in half with her enthusiasm for life, and everybody wanted her. They jostled with each other to pluck her from her cradle and puff air into her face and watch her blink and laugh.

I just wanted things to go back to the way they were.

I always knew you'd go in the end. For your wife. For your real children, the ones who shared your name. For the comforts of your life with them all. No man past his youth

95

wants to sneak around, tugging pleasure from brief, damp groans spilled across the back seat of a car. Lay-bys and street lights marking the years, and the occasional cheap-hotel-room peak, with every light in the place on and space to undress, to pretend, to move. Sometimes I'd watch you as you sat across the room from me, bent over your shoes, shirt half on, and the harder I focused on you the more indistinct you became, until I had to lean and switch the lights back off, the better to see you in the darkness.

The problem with giving someone space to move, you give them space to move away. Once I realised that she wasn't going to magic you into our lives permanently, bind you close with her soft palms and her hearty bellows, I lost all remaining belief that I would ever leave my jewellery box. I knew then that I would be that tiny ballerina forever, waiting for the lid to rise.

But I hadn't realised that forever would be over so quickly. Maybe I lost something of my previous mystique, my purity, when I became a mother. Or maybe I stopped trying once I'd accepted my role in your life. Gave up the dream and gave you up in the process.

Whichever, whatever; it's done now isn't it?

6

I was seventeen when the car struck me and brought me down to land beside my shoes. I lay in the road and looked across at the bruised black leather, tried to stretch a hand out to touch them, but couldn't.

Above me sirens shrieked and the cold blue of the sky was studded with eyes, but down here, on the road, the tarmac was warm beneath my cheek and as soft as feathers. I was turned over, shouted at. I tried to put a finger to my lips to hush the intrusion, but couldn't.

It wasn't my fault! She just stepped out in front of me!

For god's sake, don't move her! You're not supposed to move them!

Faces hung above me like balloons and then disappeared. I almost recognised some of them, though none of them seemed to recognise me. Mouths stretched so wide that I could see the scream at the back of the throat. I tried to speak to them, to ask why nobody would help me up, but couldn't.

And then there were men in uniforms and they slid me onto a board and into the back of some kind of van, and the sky disappeared but the faces didn't. I thought about my mother, waiting at home, waiting for someone other than me, and I wondered how long it would be before I could get back to her. Shouldn't somebody tell her where I was? She might be worried, or angry. Worse, she might not even notice the absence.

The world turned into a storm cloud that settled above my chest. Strip-lights pulsed like lightning-strikes. A blackbird circled above, never near enough to touch but always close enough to tantalise. I held on tight to anything within reach but when the storm faded and I raised my head to see what I was clinging to, my hands were by my sides, spread limp and pale like water lilies, resting on bed sheets.

The faces still appeared and disappeared but I didn't recognise any of them now. They smiled at me, they frowned, and sometimes they said things to each other. I knew that they must be talking about me but I couldn't hear them properly.

When I could finally speak I asked the one question that had been worrying me all of this time.

Did anyone pick up my shoes?

The face currently above me – a soft, round woman's face – lowered itself close enough for me to smell onions and coffee.

Do you know where you are, dear? Do you remember what happened?

I remembered losing my shoes, that's for sure. Maybe they didn't understand how rare and special an occasion it was to be bought a new pair of shoes. What if someone had wandered by and taken a fancy to them while I was being bundled off the road? I cleared my throat so that my voice would be louder.

My shoes?

The face smiled at me and then bobbed away. I tried to reach for the string tied to it, to bring it close again, but then another appeared. A man's face this time, velvety dark against the stiff white of his coat collars. His eyes were all pupil.

Knocked right out of them, you were. You flew through the air like a bird but unfortunately landed like a human. Both ankles broken, fractured right shoulder, concussion and a fractured cheekbone to boot. But you'll be fine. Oh, and somebody gave your shoes to your mother.

I nodded, tucked my hands under the blankets, slept. Proper sleep, without nightmares, without storm clouds. I dreamt of my parents.

They were in the front seat of a car and I was curled in the back. Pretending to nap, watching them through slit eyes. They kissed and whispered, smothered giggles into each other's necks. She climbed onto his lap, knees and lips gripping him tight, and he protested, turned his head to look at me, then held her there and hugged her close. I stretched a finger to draw a picture on the misted windows, dozed for a few moments, then the horn sounded as he groaned and jerked forward in his seat, once, twice. I sat up and started to cry. She slid away from him, reached to pat my head, looking at him and smiling. Her

flailing hand clawed air beside my face and her fingernail
scratched the corner of my ear.

When I woke I had a perfect memory of them, just as they'd
been when I was three or four. My ear stung for the rest of
the day.

The women on the ward fussed over me and gave me their
puddings. They exclaimed over my bruises and my bony arms
and legs, tapioca-grey against the bright white of my cast.
Maureen showed me photographs of her family and promised
to introduce me to her children at visiting time. Paula had
mislaid her glasses so I helped her with her crossword puzzles,
read out love stories from magazines. Jane was closest to my
age and she wanted to hear again and again about the
accident, about flying, the brief euphoria before I lost my
wings and clattered like a plastic doll into the road. They were
all so sweet, those women, and I don't remember whether I
ever asked any of them why they were in the hospital.

I gorged myself on Apple Charlotte over the next week and
spent every day swollen-stomached with indigestion, my
hipbones buried beneath flesh grown hard and round. I
wheeled myself about, ripe almost to bursting out of my
nightdress, cradling my belly and beaming at everyone who
glanced my way. I found out where the maternity ward was
and hung around the entrance, sharing coded smiles with the
expectant mothers. Finally I was asked to wear my gown
whenever I left my bed.

Little interest was taken in my play-acted pregnancy at the
time. Nobody on my own ward seemed to see my straining
stomach and nobody on the maternity ward seemed to see
beyond it. I was accepted at face value, without questions
being asked, and I'd so needed questions to be asked. If my
stay in the hospital had been any longer how many more

puddings a day would I have had to eat to maintain the illusion? And what was I hoping to achieve? I don't like to dwell on all that too much, but I think it was a phantom pregnancy in every sense; my dead baby morphed into my granny's escaped soul, and my sense that it was all somehow my own fault. Maybe. Either way, I haven't been able to eat stewed apple since.

Visitors came every day after lunch for two hours and three times a week in the early evening. I'd wait at the ward doors as soon as I'd finished the last of my puddings and stay there until every single visitor had come and then gone again. I pestered the nurses for messages and was told that my mum had definitely been at the hospital that first night, had waited while my injuries were investigated and my left ankle pinned.

White as a sheet she was. Someone fetched her in and she sat right there for hours, drinking from her flask. She had a real go at the man who hit you, shouting the odds and waking everyone up. She's rung in a few times since, to check on you. Shame you haven't got a phone at home, you could give her a ring.

They described her; the dark hair, the bitten finger nails. It certainly sounded like mum. Of course it was her, who else could it have been? And she'd been scared for me, had come to the hospital, had stayed all night to see if I was okay. I continued to wait by the door at visiting time.

A policeman came to interview me. He had the longest head I'd ever seen, his crown teetering above strands of grey like a mountain peak wreathed in cloud. He looked at me intently when he asked questions, tapped his pen against his notebook. I sweated and hid my belly beneath the bedclothes.

He told me that if the man who'd hit me with his car had to go on trial then he could get into a lot of trouble, so it was really important that I described the accident exactly as I remembered it. He told me that the man insisted that I'd stepped out into the road without looking, that he didn't have a chance to stop. I said that I didn't remember anything.

He told me that three members of the public had come forward and reported that I'd seemed agitated, distressed, was following a woman with a pram, had rushed into the road to pass a group of people who'd blocked my way. Was this true? Again I said that I didn't remember anything.

The policeman went away at lunchtime, promising to return with more questions. I bolted my lunch, followed by two puddings, and spent the afternoon on the toilet.

When I was discharged mum came to collect me. She pulled me close and started to cry. Her hair was un-brushed, her breath sour.

Oh, Fern, I was so scared. I was out of my mind with worry, I really was.

I held myself against her stiffly, stepped away and limped ahead to the taxi. Tommy helped me slide inside, his huge hands soft against my back. He rested his fingertips on the top of my head for a second, cupping my skull.

It's good to be bringing you home safe and sound, kid.

I refused to speak to mum in the car but I let her hold my hand and stroke my wrist. At home she tried to bustle around me, lead me to the sofa and thrust old magazines at me, but I stood in the middle of the room and shouted at her, swaying on my crutches, throwing the glossy peace offerings onto the floor.

You didn't visit me once! Not once, mum!

She started to cry again.

Try to be reasonable, love, how could I come? I had to wait at home in case your father came back, didn't I? Someone had to be waiting to tell him that his daughter was in hospital. It wasn't that I didn't want to be with you, but I couldn't be in two places at once, could I? I called, though, lots of times, did they tell you that? And I'm going to get a phone installed, so if something bad ever happens again you'll be able to ring and tell me.

I slumped forward on my crutches and started to laugh, squinting up at her. She gazed back at me; pleading, puzzled, hopeful. I shrugged and then winced at the pain in my shoulder.

God, you really don't get it, do you? I'll be finishing school next year and I'm getting off this island. I'm going to leave home. I'm going to leave you, mum, and I won't look back, and I hope you'll finally understand why when you're sat in this room year after year by yourself, waiting for him to come home.

She put her hands to her eyes and stood silently for a moment in front of me, then spun away with her face averted, collapsing into the doorframe for a second as she cannoned from the room. When she returned, the glass in her hand brittle with ice cubes, we both sat and watched the television, pretended that everything was fine. She brought me my dinner on a tray and I thanked the area just to the left of her head, ate without appetite, concentrated on a documentary about bees.

By the time I hobbled up to bed that night she was so drunk she couldn't be shifted from the sofa. I draped a coat over her shoulders and left her there.

*

I don't ask mum's permission to sift through every drawer and cupboard in the house. She follows me from room to room, snorting contempt, but she doesn't stop me, not even when I clamber up the flaking stepladder to the attic and start to hurl bulging carrier bags onto the landing. She scuttles out of the way and retreats back downstairs then, feeding the banister through her fist and lowering herself one muttered step at a time, as if scared that I'll sneak up behind her and give her a shove, just for the hell of it. The phone starts to screech as she's halfway down and she lets out a startled yelp and stumbles, but regains her balance and composure, continues on.

The naked bulb suspended from the central beam in the attic tumbles shadow across the narrow space, creating angles that don't exist. Tarnished metal chests loom from the corners and then retreat as light briefly glances over them and swings away. A spider, rendered grotesque and huge, shifts on a pile of blankets. I keep a wary eye on it as I sort through boxes. In a cracked, tan leather folder I find Granny Ivy's marriage certificate and mum's birth certificate. I rip the thin paper as I spread it open and tear mum's name down the centre.

There are fat little parcels of letters from people I've never heard of *(We must meet up next year, all my love Doreen. Thank you so much for the pickles, Arthur ate half a jar in one sitting! Love Janet)* and one from the great-aunt, just a couple of sentences on unlined paper, as brisk and unsentimental as my memory of her. *Ivy, I got your letter and I'll do as you ask. Please don't contact me again. Rose.*

If mum ever corresponded with anyone, ever, she must have destroyed the evidence a long time ago. It's as if she had no past. There's nothing of hers at all up here, though there are plenty of my old drawings and school reports, sorted into date order and inserted into paper folders. I know without asking that it was my granny, not my mum, who would have done that.

The spider has disappeared the next time I look over and so I decide to retreat to the landing to sort through the bags there. My enthusiasm is starting to ebb, last night's angry determination segueing into a mild nausea that, since I got pregnant, hits me whenever my stomach's empty. I call out to mum but she doesn't answer.

Granny Ivy's household accounts, her payslips from the post office, lots and lots of old till receipts. I rummage for a while and then look at my watch. It's nearly time for lunch. There's still no sound from beneath me. It's as if mum's holding her breath down there. I wade through the bags and paper to check she's still alive.

She's in her chair, staring out of the window. She pretends not to have heard me come in and flinches dramatically.

'Everything okay, mum? I'll make us some pasta soon for lunch and then I'll start on the dresser in the kitchen, so if there's anything in there you want to hide now's your chance.'

She remains frigidly fixated on the window but there's an almost-smile tugging at her mouth. She looks sly, pleased with herself. 'Haven't found anything yet, then? I knew you wouldn't.'

I take her empty glass and tilt it towards her. 'Another water?'

She looks up at me, lips thinned to nothing. 'Oh, that would be lovely, Fern. Thanks so much.' Her hands are shaking.

The power that I have over her is a visible thing. It hangs in the tremble of her fingers, hardens in the grim clench of her cheek muscles as she refuses to ask for that one thing she wants above all else. The nausea swells inside me. I can try telling myself that this is purely for her own good but I know that I'm denying her her only solace just because I can, because it's the most effective way of punishing her.

I try to soften my voice, smooth out the mocking edge it's so easy to use with her. 'Just a couple more bags then I'll be done upstairs. And, no, I haven't found anything yet. If I hadn't seen dad with my own eyes I'd think you were making him up. But then, if you weren't sat right here I'd be doubting your existence as well, you've done such a good job of scrubbing yourself right off the face of the earth. Are you sure you don't work as a spy?'

I really can't help myself.

The last two bags are full of what looks like fabric. Granny Ivy's unfinished sewing? I empty them out over the carpet and pounce on a lovely green velvet bag. There's no way mum's getting her hands on that. I undo the clasp and pull out the contents. Envelopes, all addressed to the great-aunt and all in Granny Ivy's handwriting. I recognise the spiky, flourished lettering, the ferociously stabbed *t*'s. They all smell faintly of the lavender she sprinkled over everything.

I take them into my bedroom and spread them across the bed, one by one.

Dear Rose,   June 22nd '42

I won't offer any excuses; I can't imagine you'd want to hear them. And I won't even say that I'm sorry because I'd do it again tomorrow. But I do regret hurting you. I do regret that.

I hope the parents are doing everything they can to be a comfort to you. I hope mother's stopped crying by now, though it's only been a few hours so I can't imagine she has. She really did turn the most extraordinary shade of red didn't she? I thought for a moment that she'd collapse right there in front of me, and that might just have been too much for my conscience. Thankfully I didn't have to find out.

Edgar is just discovering that he doesn't have sea legs, the poor thing. I, on the other hand, am calm and sickness free, which is remarkable considering my situation. Hardly the most romantic of elopements, so I hope you will take some pleasure from that. We've barely spoken a word since we left you, and I was so eager to get him away from the island before he could change his mind I forgot to take my blue coat. You can have it, I know you've always wanted it.

I also left my crystals. They're in a grey velvet bag under my bed. Please bury them, but don't touch them with bare skin. I hadn't rinsed them in salt water so they'll still hold a charge from the last charm.

I sit here on deck, shivering in my thin dress, imagining you all gathered around the stove in the kitchen and dripping poison onto the table. But at least mother will have the satisfaction of being proved right about me! I just hope she's not gloating too much at your expense. She always prophesised I'd create a scandal that would bring our good name to its knees, didn't she?

But it could have been worse, couldn't it? We could have waited until after you and Edgar were married and then ran away together. Or we could have carried on an affair through the years, with me as the spinster elder sister always at your home or making excuses for him to visit me. There's only so many leaky taps that require a man's attention before his wife starts to get suspicious.

I do wish we hadn't left it so close to the wedding though, I do really. And you looked so beautiful in your dress, the last time you tried it on. Did you know that I wanted to rip it off you? Did you ever glance up from the mirror and see the jealousy on my face as I hovered behind you? I always tried not to think of you as a rival but you were so perfect in your white lace. I couldn't understand how he could want me when he could have you. But nevertheless here we all are.

If it hadn't been for the baby maybe I wouldn't have taken him, or maybe he wouldn't have come, but I don't believe that. Even before I found out about her (and it will be a her, I sense it) we talked about his leaving you and about us being together properly, in daylight. It was just a matter of time and courage, and this bump beneath my dress gave us the latter.

I can imagine what you're thinking, and no I didn't. I've never planned anything in my life, you of all people know that, though I suppose that the frequency of our meetings and the intensity of our love meant that the odds were stacked in favour of me falling pregnant. But I didn't plan it. Honest, Rose, I didn't.

As to the other thing that I'm sure you've been wondering about: yes I did. There, does that make you feel better? I didn't play fair! But from the first moment I saw him, that afternoon you brought him home to show him off, I loved him. I couldn't take my eyes from his hedgehog hands, his fingers bristling with splinters and his palms so pink and tender. I wanted to close my mouth over them, feel for each of those splinters with my tongue and pull them out with my teeth. So I used a love spell on him, and for that I _am_ sorry. Neither of us will know whether I could have won him through feminine wiles alone, and if I had the time again I wouldn't put it to the test. I couldn't risk losing him. You see, I love him more than anything. More than myself, more than the island, and more than you.

I have to check on him now so I'm going to finish this letter. It'll take ages to find him in the dark, and we've been told we can't even light a candle as the glow will carry so far. I'll post this as soon as we get to the mainland, and I'll write again when we have an address. Please excuse my scrawl, I only have moonlight to guide me.

The island's going to miss its charmer, and I'm going to miss the island. I'm going to miss you too, if I'm allowed to say that. When the war is over we may come back. As to our private war, Rosy Rose, please give me a sign when hostilities are suspended and you can forgive me. I know it can't be soon, but I hope it will happen.

With my love,

Ivy

Dearest Rose,   Oct 13th '42

Sad news. We lost our little girl, seven months in and on the night of our wedding. The nurse at the hospital let me wrap her up in the white shawl I'd crocheted and hold her for a while before they took her away. She was so beautiful, Rose, she reminded me of you. Her eyes were shut so I couldn't see their colour but I know they were brown. Her lashes were longer than mine, they lay as feathery fine as peacock's tails on her cheeks, and her lids shimmered like the insides of scallop shells. I felt such an urge to crouch on the bed with my legs spread wide and push her back inside me. My body her coffin. Surely she'd be happier nestled in the cushion of my flesh than wrapped in wood and given to the earth? But they took her as soon as I tried and I haven't seen her since.

I'm still in the hospital, though I should be allowed to go home tomorrow. I had septicaemia after I lost her and I was almost lost too. If it weren't for Edgar I'd have happily followed my little girl into the after world but he never let me forget him, howling at me to live and causing such a scene in the corridor there was very nearly a fight.

She took a breath in, just one, before she died and so technically was a living birth and entitled to be baptised. I refused; do you think that was wrong of me? The nurses said that she would be cast into limbo if I didn't, but I still said no. I couldn't tell them that if her soul's floating in limbo then there's a chance I can reach out to her and console her, maybe even tether her and bring her back to me, but if she's in heaven then she's gone forever. Once those gates are shut they stay closed.

I had the same dream three nights in a row before she died. There was a time when I would have paid heed to such dreams but over the last few months I've become complacent with love and sluggish with happiness and I can only blame myself for that. You were my dream, Rose, and when I think of it now I can't imagine how I could have ignored its warning.

It was your wedding day. You stood in our garden at home (I mean <u>our</u> garden, our childhood garden), dressed in your white lace, your hair tucked into a veil. You were marrying Edgar. I watched you watch him and I felt overcome with joy for you both despite my own love for him. It was wonderful.

It started to rain and I stepped forward and held you in my arms, trying to shield you from the worst of the downpour. No matter how I covered you with my body you got wetter and wetter, but you rested against me so serenely, eyes shut, not minding the damage to your dress. I stayed dry and though you started to shiver I was warm.

When it stopped raining we both undressed and redressed in each other's clothing, so that you too would be warm, on your wedding day. And then Edgar took my hand and led me through the garden and out of the gate. When we reached the road I looked back and you were standing in my violet silk, your ruined veil sodden around your face, watching us walk away from you. In your hand, in place of a bouquet, you held the white shawl I'd crocheted for my little girl. It trailed from your fingers and down onto the ground. <u>Into</u> the ground, like a thread connecting you to the earth.

It feels as if we've been cursed.

Our house is sweet, though small, but with a lovely little garden at the back. It would have been perfect. I've planted two delicate pink rose bushes, one either side of the door, so that I will be reminded of you every time I return home. Edgar has found work in a sawmill and he whittles tiny figurines for me in his breaks. I have a collection of dancing animals on the sill above the fireplace and intricate trees in miniature. I love the symmetry of that; trees felled and then re-born as carvings of themselves.

You would hate it here, the land doesn't ever seem to end. It scares me, the thought that I could walk and walk and never reach the end of it.

I think of you often, Rose, and always with a heart full of love. We never speak about you and I have to tell you that we still don't regret what we did. Not yet anyway. I adore him more with each passing day, and even in the midst of this tragedy the touch of his fingertips against my neck pulls my stomach up into my throat and butterflies fly from my mouth.

I hope you have it in you to pity me and mourn your little niece. We'll bury her next week. I was going to name her Fern.

Our wedding night was a dead infant curled on bloodied bed sheets and our honeymoon was a hospital ward. It's as if God's punishing me.

With love,

Ivy

My Dear Rose,   April 10ᵗʰ '45

We're coming home! Well, not quite, so don't start packing your bags just yet. We're going to move to Spur, only a few hour's ferry ride away, and on a clear day I will be able to stand at the southern-most point and see our island. My island. Imagine that! I've got tears in my eyes at the mere thought of it. Of course, if you were ever to let me know that you forgive me then nothing would stop me from returning home properly, back to Sorel and to you.

With Edgar's training in cabinet making he shouldn't want for work and I've grown used to cleaning other people's houses, so all we need now is a home. Edgar will travel there later this month to find us one. He's as excited as I am to be returning to island life and I think he actually prefers the idea of returning to settle somewhere different, close enough to home to feel secure but without the memories and complications of actually <u>being</u> home. He'd never say that though, knowing as he does how much I love Sorel.

We won't miss our life here on the mainland, though on reflection there have been some good points. I'm pals with a lovely lady called Janet who has a little four-year-old girl (such a beautiful child though even naughtier than I used to be, if you can believe that!). We met when we were queuing for meat in the village (of course, there wasn't any to be had), and we've been thick as thieves since.

I'm knitting you a scarf for your birthday. You have no idea how hard it was to get wool in that colour! I had to trade my fat ration with Mrs Mills from two doors up. That woman is such a hoarder. I hope pink is still your favourite. I'll wear it for you, and keep it safe until I see you again. I have to believe I'll see you again one day.

It's strange but when I picture you it's always as a girl, years younger than you were when we last saw each other. Maybe I simply want to return to a kinder, more innocent time in our lives, before fate and adulthood drove their wedge between us? It scares me sometimes to think that if I saw you now I wouldn't even recognise you, I've become so blinkered. Wherever I go I scan the crowds for a child's figure when I should be on the lookout for a woman's. I'm sure in my heart that couldn't be possible, I'd always recognise my own sister, but in another few years, Rose, when time has carved new faces for us both, it might prove true.

I've recovered from the last miscarriage, and the doctor doesn't see why I can't carry a baby to full term in the future, but three pregnancies lost does make me fear that Edgar and I will never be blessed with children. He bears the pain silently and is such a comfort. I, on the other hand, wail and screech and am furious with the world for weeks afterwards, throwing myself around the house in a fury. I'm sure you can imagine the scenes.

I've felt queasy these last few days so I'm hopeful that I may be expecting again, but it's too early and I'm too nervous to say anything to anybody but you just yet.

Can I tell you another secret? It's not one I can share with anyone here. Only an islander would really understand, and you particularly, knowing me as you do. Edgar and I had a terrible argument a couple of weeks ago; he returned home from work for his lunch earlier than I was expecting and I was using my moonstones to cast a charm to ensure safe pregnancy. He was livid, as I'd promised when we married that I'd never practise spells again. I think my position as the island's charmer had always made him nervous and he can't separate a little white magic from the nightmare image he holds in his mind of a wart-nosed witch delivering hellfire from atop a broomstick. I've tried to tell him that my work never involved anything more exciting than curing trapped wind and lame cows (and, yes, performing the odd love spell), but he can be obstinate and unyielding, and on this subject particularly so.

We don't argue often but this one went around and around for hours. Eventually, I lost my temper and became as unreasonable as he. We went to bed in silence and awoke the next day in silence. When he left for work I turned straight to my book and performed a charm for forgetting. Is that terrible of me? The worst thing is I don't even feel guilty because when he came home that night he brought flowers and apologies and we've been like newly-weds ever since. I'd promised to burn my spell book but I've hidden it instead, buried in the garden next to the forget-me-nots. I was steeling myself to lie to him but he hasn't mentioned it again. It really is like he's dropped the whole argument from his memory. I am determined to do as he wants though, as it would make him happy and making him happy is what I live for. I ripped the spell from my book and enclose it with this letter so that I'm not ever tempted to use it again.

Just think, within a few months at most I'll be less than thirty miles from you, and separated only by air and water. I reckon I could even swim that distance (well, very nearly) if I had to, and you needed me.

I hope the parents are well, and have moved past the stage of cursing the day I was born.

I hope you have.

With my love to you,

Ivy

Spell To Forget

Write down that which you wish to forget onto
a twist of paper.
Dry and powder two knuckle-sized pieces of
Valerian Root.
Place in a bowl with two sprigs of
Crushed Rosemary and a torn
Sage leaf.
Add the paper.
Set the mix alight and breathe deeply of
the smoke it produces.
Forgetfulness will begin to enter your psyche.
When the smoke has cleared take to your bed
and when you awake your troubled thoughts
will have fled.
You may then discard the ashes.

To Make Another Forget:

This should only be attempted with caution and after
much consideration for this involves meddling with
another's mind.
Add to the bowl a photograph of the one
whom you wish to be relieved of their memory.
Or draw a picture and name their image.
Set the mix alight but do not breathe in the smoke.
Take the ashes after the flames have died
and bury them beneath a sapling oak.
Ensure that they are not ever disturbed.

Dearest Rose,   January 8th '46

We have a daughter! Born last week after an excruciating labour that, at times, I thought was going to kill us both. We're calling her Iris, do you like that name? She's a crotchety little thing, barely opens her eyes before she's yelling for something, and is as velvety-wrinkled as the inside of a pug's ear. Do you remember the time we dressed that unfortunate little creature of Mrs Ellis' in my doll's dress and bonnet, and it ran away before I could take them back off? She refused to admit there was a funny side when she saw her precious poppet shuffling up the garden path like a Victorian matron! She wouldn't hear of you being involved either, as I recall, the fault had to be all mine.

But back to Iris. She has all her fingers and toes, and is in the rudest health, so I'm informed. She's certainly the loudest baby in the nursery and is already attracting disapproving glances from the nurses! 'Baby Gilbert, I'll bet,' whisper the other mothers, smugly nursing their own floppy, subdued babes. Can you believe some women are chloroformed when they are in labour? What that must do to those tiny hearts and souls I dread to think. I refused everything but the catnip tea I'd brought in with me, which, I have to say, did less than I was hoping to relieve the pain. I hadn't realised there'd be so much blood. I've been kept to my bed for the last week and I don't mind the rest actually.

Edgar was made to stay in the corridor and he had a terrible time listening to me screaming. He told me afterwards that there were quite a collection of expectant fathers in that night, some pacing the floor alongside him but others playing poker and chatting up the nurses. Can you imagine that? Edgar said that they're probably the ones who are on their fourth or fifth child and joked that when we get to that number he'll be so relaxed that he'll buy a pack of cards for himself!

He is delighted with Iris and spends more time at the nursery mooning over her than by my bed, but I forgive him that. I wanted to name her after you but he wasn't happy about it so Rose is to be one of her middle names.

The snow's piled up outside the windows here, so you must have snow on Sorel too. There's even ice crusting the sea shore, and on Christmas morning when Edgar was walking back from church a bird dropped from the sky and landed at his feet. It must have frozen to death. He brought it home to show me and I held it in my mittens and vowed to share my bread with its fellows every day from now on. I would have buried it if the ground hadn't been as hard as iron, so it went on the compost heap instead. There's a nice collection of people at church, and they're very accepting of us even though I sense some of them recognise our name and know about my past. I think my bulging dress helped with that somewhat, as nobody wants to judge a pregnant woman too harshly. We'll have Iris christened there in the spring.

I can hear my precious girl yelling for her supper so I have to go. Oh, the noise! She really is a tyrant. They'll be glad to see the back of the pair of us here.

Much love to you, as always.

Ivy

Ps.

I've heard your news, Rose. Married! The lady who works in the grocer's has a cousin who lives on Sorel and she said that this cousin dressed your hair last summer when you married. I was too taken aback to hide my shock well and she clearly wanted to probe but Iris started screaming and I was able to escape.

It's strange, and so sad, that neither of us were at the other's wedding. Do you remember when we were young and used to dress up in mother's bridal gown, we both promised that the other would be our maiden of honour when the day came? It was unthinkable then that it could be any other way. I should have been by your side on your wedding day, helping you on with your dress and kissing your forehead when I adjusted your veil. I should have been there.

But I'm so happy for you, I really am, and I hope with all my heart that he's worthy of you and you're happy too.

With love,

Ivy

My Dearest Rose,   September 14th '52

I'm snatching a moment between topping and tailing four big bowls of gooseberries, ready for pies and jam. Two bowls down now, two to go … My back aches from bending over the folding table, which I've set up in the garden to catch the evening sun. Iris is standing at the far end, staring over the fence down towards the main road at the end of the lane. She's waiting for a glimpse of cars, and though barely more than one will pass in an hour she'll stand patiently and wait for an entire afternoon at a time. Strange child. To think only a year ago she would have had to be lifted to see over the fence.

I'm pregnant again. To be frank, I can barely summon any excitement this time. Two lost since Iris and god knows how many more yet to lose. Sometimes, when I lie in bed and can't sleep, I stare into the darkness and see them all gathered before me. Their souls flicker like fairies candles, circling the night above my head, each a separate remonstration before merging into one faint parade of light and then fading. There must be something terribly wrong with my womb, that it cannot cradle an infant beyond a couple of months before rejecting it in the cruellest way. My only comfort is the knowledge that this cannot go on for too much longer, as I'm surely past the height of my fertile years.

I heard from Mrs Avery at the grocer's (My pocket spy. Now that I've abandoned all pretence at dignity and beg for news she delights in feeding me what titbits she can glean), about father's death last winter. It was a shock more to the senses than the emotions, the way news of death will always shock, but I haven't cried at all and feel no real grief. We were never close, though, were we? Even you had to dance to his tune and I always felt as if I were more of an imposition on his time than anything else. I do wonder if he mellowed over the years, and I do hope that the end wasn't painful for him. How did mother take it? And how did you, Rosy Rose?

I've managed to save our beautiful oak from Edgar's axe (the oak that whispers to me when I go into the back garden to hang out the washing), though it took some persuasion. He said that it would one day prove to be a menace as it's too close to the house, which may well be true, but I know that he was really measuring its size and calculating the weight of logs it would provide. So we've compromised and he's cut down the ash instead, which I don't mind as it partially blocked my view from the kitchen window anyway.

I'm going to finish this letter as it's time Iris left her post at the garden fence and came indoors to wash her hands before tea. Tommy, the lovely young lad who delivers our milk, let me have a quart of thick yellow cream this morning, so we're going to have it with gooseberry tart if I ever finish this damn topping and tailing.

Thinking of you.

Ivy

Rose,   March 19th '54

He's gone. He's gone. He's gone. He's gone. He's gone.

No matter how many times I repeat it, it won't sink in. He's gone. Even though I sit here with his hand cold in mine and the stench from his decayed lungs sticky on my skin I can feel a twitch of fingers against my own. If I lean close that surely was a trickle of breath against my cheek? But he's gone.

I'm writing this to you while I wait for the doctor. I've sent Iris to the neighbours. She doesn't need to see her father like this. It will be a while before Dr Collins arrives for he prioritises the living over the dead, and rightly so. I hope he takes all day. Once he's here, and Edgar's gone, I'll have to busy myself with all of those tasks required of a widow. There'll be visitors, and endless cups of tea to drink, and a funeral to arrange. But for now it's just us. It feels so familiar in this room, it'll be strange to finally go back to the old bedroom, and even stranger to sleep in a bed again. This was supposed to be the nursery for our second child that never was. I can still see the faded jade outlines of an owl, a cat and a boat repeated over and over across the walls. I didn't ever think that the ghost that will now haunt it is to be the ghost of the one person I've loved more than any other.

I thought I'd be relieved when we reached this moment, but I'm not. The end was bad but I'd have it all back again, make him suffer again, to have him with me. I suppose I've always been selfish like that.

He doesn't even look like him any more. His face is withered and sunken as if he's struggled through decades of pain. His lips have disappeared. His chest, which used to be such a great comforting slab of muscle, has collapsed inwards and is now just gristle on bone.

The last few weeks were the worst. When he moved into this room it was only so that I could get some sleep at night but I think he left his soul behind in our marriage bed and he just gave up. I followed him with this chair and made it comfortable with cushions and knew we were in trouble when he didn't argue with me.

It was terrible, Rose, the way the tumour inside him feasted on his body. At first just a nibble here and a nibble there then larger bites when it got a taste for him until it eventually opened its great wide mouth and bared its sharp teeth and swallowed him down. And left me with nothing.

Iris wouldn't even come to the bedroom door in the final days, she was so scared of him. I hit her last week because I caught her holding the neck of her dress to her nose when she was on the landing, her face all screwed up. I hit her as hard as I could across the cheek and then pulled the dress down and made her breathe in huge gulps of air. I was screaming at her and she was screaming back at me and I would have hit her again but he fell out of bed in his agitation to reach us and it brought me to my senses. I went to find her once he was settled back into bed but she wouldn't look at me and she hasn't spoken to me since.

His fingers are starting to claw a little now and there's a peculiar hardness in his limbs as if he's been packed with straw. What was the straw man lacking? The straw man from Oz? It wasn't courage. I can't remember.

I've been fantasising for weeks about visiting that so-called specialist Edgar went to see on the mainland and sliding a knife into his back, right through, until I can see the tip of it poking through his tie at the front. He was fine until he went there. He had a cough, I know he had a cough, but he was fine.

He couldn't say much by the end so we'd just sit together and I'd hold his hand. He stopped eating and then he stopped drinking. He didn't take his eyes from my face. As soon as they opened they'd fix on me and they said everything his mouth couldn't.

He tried not to take his tablets, he didn't want to lose a moment of the time we had left, but I begged him and in the end he gave in. By that stage I don't think they did much for the pain but I have to think that they did something for it.

The sun's high in the sky now and the primroses I've kept on the bedside table are soaked with light. I think he really is gone, Rose. But at least I kept that promise I made him all those years ago. No spells. No charms. They may have helped him to live (and that I won't dwell on because it's not something I'll ever know) but at the cost of betraying his trust.

The friends we've made around here have been wonderful, making sure we don't starve and taking Iris to play with their children. You could never have called us a particularly sociable couple, we didn't need the company of other people when we had each other, but I'm grateful for the support now and reckon I'll be even more grateful over the coming months.

Rose, the reason for our estrangement is lying dead and cold before me and my heart is torn open. It feels as if some wild beast has it between its paws and is shredding it with claws of glass. He was yours before he was mine and in a different world or if you'd had a different sister he might still be yours now. Maybe he'd still be alive if I'd left him alone?

Please think of me. Please think of him. He really was the best man I've ever known.

Ivy

Dear Rose,   March 21st '64

Well, another anniversary endured and now passed. I can't believe it's been ten years since he died. Ten years! The primroses I've planted around his grave are coming into bloom and I think they'll do him proud this year.

This insomnia hasn't got any better. Last week my brain was so fogged I miscalculated a lady's change at the post office and she really took me to task over it, as if I'd deliberately set out to rob her of a few miserable pennies! Mr David said I should go to the doctor's surgery and ask for tablets. He's worried that my work will continue to suffer. But the only possible thing the doctor could give me to help me sleep would be my husband back in my bed, and the last I heard he wasn't a miracle worker, (far from it). I'm almost getting used to the sleeplessness now, anyway, it's been so long.

Word has got around that I'm a charmer and when I eye the queues I can tell immediately the ones who are waiting for a book of stamps and the ones waiting for assistance of a more personal nature. A few people have even come to the house but I gave them short shrift. There's been nothing too exciting (the usual water infections, sickly infants and ant infestations), and you'll be pleased to know, Rose, that I refuse to perform love spells.

From my seat at the kitchen table I can see Iris standing by the garden gate, dressed up to the nines and swinging my old sequined handbag, the one that Edgar bought me when we were first married. She's not even wearing her cardigan. She's waiting for her gentleman friend, though how she ever knows he's coming I just can't work out. More hope than actual information, I suspect. As far as I can gather (and she tells me nothing) she has no direct way of contacting him, so either they have a 'drop' (I knew I shouldn't have let her watch those spy movies at the theatre when she was a young girl) where they exchange notes, or she simply decides on any random morning that today will be her lucky day and gets herself ready and waiting. It's starting to spit with rain now but she won't come inside, not even to fetch a coat.

I have my own theories about this man of hers but she won't so much as mention his name to me these days. I met him last month and it only took one good look at him to know what his game was. My eyes are still sharp enough to spot a married man a mile off! He was very polite, I couldn't fault his manners, but he smelt funny. He's from the mainland and said he travels here to meet clients. He works for a pharmaceutical company and tried to make it sound very exotic but he's just a jumped up travelling salesman from the sound of it. He reeks of wealth and is certainly handsome, but he's got to be fifteen years older than her. And she won't let poor Tommy have a look-in no matter how he moons around her.

He, the oh-so-flash one, became very shifty when I started asking him questions. He's very clever at not actually answering anything asked of him, whilst making it seem as if he's as open and honest as the next man. He was itching to leave after about half an hour, I think he knew I had his number, and he hasn't been back inside the house since.

I want to sit Iris down and tell her that he's married but fear that'll just make her hate me the more. She was always a dissatisfied girl, but it was only after Edgar died that things between us really broke down. I was so consumed with my own loss that I didn't allow her a moment to express her own grief and now I think it's too late. I guarded my widowhood and my memories too jealously. I still do, if I'm honest.

She's turned eighteen now and shows no interest in getting a job or doing anything much at all. There's always work at the soap factory but she turns her nose up at the thought of it. I know she believes this man will be her knight in shining armour and sweep her off to exotic lands, but even a fool can see that he wants her to stay right where she is.

She's still waiting out there, and it's starting to rain hard now. I'll take her a coat. Not that I'll get thanked for it.

With love, as always.

Ivy

Dearest Rose,   11th Dec '66

I'm a grandmother! Oh, and she's beautiful. I held her in my arms before anyone else and in that instant it was as if my heart had come back to life. She's going to be called Fern, at my insistence. She would have shared a birth date with my own lost Fern, if my Fern had survived to be born, and so the parallels couldn't be overlooked. Iris says she doesn't mind and I can call her what I like.

Who would have thought that there would be such a happy ending? If you'd told me five months ago that I would fall in love with the child I would probably have turned you out of the house. It makes me ashamed to think how difficult I made things for Iris when she was pregnant.

Needless to say, he hasn't been to visit his daughter, though as there's no way she can get a message to him I suppose we shouldn't expect him. But she does expect him, I know she does, and she called out for him throughout the birth. Poor Tommy, who came to collect us, looked sick with worry. It was as if he were the father. He carried Iris up the hospital steps and kept her in his arms even when a wheelchair was brought. I think he would have carried her all the way into the delivery room and stayed by her side if he'd been given a chance.

She's upstairs resting at the moment; the labour really took it out of her. She barely stirs even when Fern starts up for a feed. I should really speak to her about weaning Fern off the breast and onto bottles so that I don't have to disturb her every time my little one needs a feed.

I do wonder if she's depressed, or maybe pining for him. It's been a couple of months since I heard his car in the lane outside. But what did she think was going to happen, for pity's sake? A man doesn't leave the wife just because the mistress has his child. And besides, he may well have half a dozen legitimate children for all we know, and not be overly impressed at the thought of adding another baby to his bloodline. But it's not even as if she's ever shown an interest in finding out. If I were in her position I wouldn't rest until I knew everything there was to know about his life away from me. Everything.

So, this may well be the last we see of Mr Flash Suits, and I for one won't shed a tear at the thought. There was a time, last year, when I actually considered casting a love spell to bind him to her and I came very close to doing it as well. But despite her misery and my longing to make her happy something stopped me. I'm so glad now that it did. If I had, and it worked, they'd be together somewhere away from here and I wouldn't have the joy of raising Fern.

So you're a great-aunt now, Rose, as well as an aunt. How old we're getting. My hair's more grey than black these days, and my knees creak when I stoop down. But I don't mind any of it really. I've had my youth, and I had Edgar, and now I have Fern. I just hope that things can be easier between Iris and me in the future. I'm determined to try my hardest with her and she's going to need me a lot more than she realises.

The warmth from the stove is releasing the scents from the dried fruit and spices I've got piled on the table, and the kitchen smells like the gingerbread cottage! It's even weaving its way into Fern's dreams, she's starting to stir and snuffle now. I've hung a muslin bag from her crib and filled it with chips of tourmaline, to keep her safe. There's also a small chunk of amethyst under her mattress, by her feet. I was worried that Iris would scoff and insist I take them away but she hasn't even noticed.

I promise to think of you on Christmas morning, with much love. I might even take a walk after lunch so that I can see Sorel and feel closer to you all. Of course, that will depend on whether Fern allows me an hour to myself.

With lots of love,

Ivy

Dearest Rose,   July 8th '71

So, mother's dead.

In a way I'm glad that it takes three days for the ferry to spit out Sorel's Evening Post on Spur's shore. If I'd known in time for the funeral then maybe I would have considered travelling over. Maybe I would have thought I should have. And that's not how I ever imagined a return home to my island.

Fern is grubbing about in the dirt at my feet as I write this and keeps bringing me worms to sex and tiny beetles to heal. I swear she has a touch of my own charm. They say it skips a generation and shows itself only on the female side so maybe I should be uncovering my spell book and wrapping it up for her for her next birthday.

Iris is away with <u>him</u>. I have no idea where they went but she packed her weekend bag so I don't expect her back tonight. I imagine he takes her to Sorel when they spend the night away, so you may well have passed them in town. It is strange to think they might even now be walking past our childhood home, without so much as a glance through the garden gate. Iris has never expressed much interest in my family (somewhat to my relief, as an honest telling of all that would have been difficult), though she was curious to see so many of his relatives at Edgar's funeral and I would have encouraged her in pursuing those bonds if there had been the slightest encouragement from them. As it was, they came to the service but barely acknowledged either of us, and we've never heard a thing since.

I'm more than happy to look after my little pumpkin while Iris gallivants with that man but I do wish they'd include her sometimes. I worry that Iris blames her for the sorry state of her life. If she'd remained childless then she wouldn't now have to work at the soap factory to bring an income into the home and she'd be free. Having his child has kept her locked in a box, which has worked out well for him as he has the key, but not for her. And not for Fern either.

I can't see an end to it now. It makes me gloomy to think of the years stretching ahead of us all: Iris losing her youth and her looks, the visits from him becoming more and more perfunctory, and Fern having to witness it all. It's so important for a child to have love and respect for their father, but how can she respect a man she barely knows and who sweeps down upon her home whenever the whim takes him, to snatch her mother away from her? The last time he came into the house she actually attacked him and I'm ashamed to say that I didn't scold her at all for it. Quite the opposite, if I'm honest. I know that won't have helped the situation any but the sight of his face all screwed up and scarlet was delicious!

There were times after Fern was born when I'd wake in the night, stiff with fear at the thought that she might actually be the prompt he needed to leave his wife, but his visits are as irregular as ever. I have to assume that they will continue with this affair until it wears them both out, and Iris is already showing a mental fragility that concerns me. She measures her life by his visits and mopes the rest of the time. I've caught her muttering to herself more than once, as if she's offering up prayers to the gods. She leaps out of her skin when she sees me, as if disturbed in the act of something intimate or forbidden.

It's nearly time for tea and I've promised the little pumpkin that she can have scones topped with as much cream as she can fit into her stomach. She's over by the oak now, hugging it as hard as she can. She seems to love it as much as I do, and as much as Iris used to when she was young. She's filthy from her fingertips to her elbows so I'll need to get her scrubbed before she can make a start on the scones.

I'll think of mother tonight when I'm in bed, and I'll think of you too. I hope her death hasn't affected you too badly.

With my love,

Ivy

*

Over lunch I'm so quiet that mum's interest is piqued. She's not used to being out-sulked. She sips the juice I gave her and watches me stir the food around my plate.

'You've got to eat. There's more than just you to think about now. Though I don't blame you, this pasta tastes funny.'

I knew I hadn't crushed the tablet properly. To distract her, I bring up the subject of the great-aunt, though decide mum doesn't need to know about the letters.

'Do you know why Granny Ivy and her sister never spoke?' I ask. 'Was there an argument?'

She shrugs, disinterested. 'Some trouble when they were young. Something unforgivable your granny did, no doubt.

Why are you so interested, anyway? She's never been interested in us.'

'But she is family. Don't you think it would be nice to put all that aside and make an effort while we still can? Does she still live on Sorel?'

Mum wipes pasta sauce from her plate with a piece of bread then drops it, uneaten, and pushes her chair back. 'I have no idea. Family is more than just blood and bones, Fern. I know why you're curious, I was the same when I was pregnant with you, but take my advice and save yourself some heartache; the only family that matters are the ones who will take you in no matter what you've done, and never ask questions.'

She turns and leaves the room. I follow her through to the lounge. 'Wait a second, mum, so by that definition Granny Ivy, your mother, is in the inner circle of your version of family.'

She settles herself in her armchair and turns the television on. 'I'm going to have my nap now. Could you wake me at four, please?'

'Admit it. She kept you fed and safe, she looked after you and your child and she left you, us both, well provided for. She may have asked a few questions that you might not have wanted to answer but she didn't turn her back on you. So, she was your family. The moment she died you started drinking. It was as if she was your lynch pin.'

Mum turns her face away and pulls her blanket up to her neck. 'Why so sentimental all of a sudden, Fern? Yes, all right, she was family. Of course she was family. Now, I'm tired and I want to have a rest if that's okay with you.'

The yawn she forces is as infectious as it is irritating and I think how nice it would be to go to bed and shut my eyes for a while. Instead, I leaf through the letters again and then dial directory enquiries for the telephone number that corresponds with the most recent address. It's about fifteen years old but I may as well try it.

The voice that answers is sharp. 'Yes?'

I imagine a meal cooling on a table, a bus needing to be caught, and stumble over my request. 'I'm really sorry to bother you, but I was trying to trace a relative of mine, a Rose Atkins ...'

'She doesn't live here any more.'

I wince into the receiver. 'Is there any chance you might know where she lives now?'

The briefest of pauses, then: 'I think she went into that new nursing home that opened at the top of town. But that was a few years ago now.'

I take the name of the nursing home and look through the phone book until I find the number. The person that answers the phone this time is even more brisk. As I ask my questions I push the kitchen door shut even though I can hear the gentle purr of mum snoring.

I'm forced to wait while a manager is summoned, but it's finally confirmed that the great aunt does indeed live there and is willing to see me. As I juggle pen and paper to take directions mum growls in her sleep, breath whining through her nostrils. I peer through the crack in the door and watch her shift and open her eyes briefly, then moan and resettle. For a second I'm tempted to ask if they have any vacancies for foul tempered alcoholics, but I settle instead for arranging to visit the next afternoon. I can always check the rooms out while I'm there anyway, and maybe take home a brochure to leave on the kitchen table the next time mum plays me up.

She's smiling from the moment she opens her eyes. 'Oh, Fern, I had such a lovely dream,' she tells me as I massage her clawed fingers and then reinsert her arm into her sling. She pats at me with her free hand, trying to keep me close, and I sit and listen. There's never much variation to her dreams: she's always young and beautiful, it's always summertime, and my father is always opening the garden gate or stretching out a hand to her. I'm never in them. I do suspect that they're more waking dreams or conscious fantasy than anything else because, come on, nobody has such perfect wish-fulfilment dreams over and over again. Do they? I know if I did then I'd spend a lot more time in bed. But maybe I'm just cynical because I'm piqued not to ever be given so much as a walk-on part.

I smile back at her, glad her mood has improved so dramatically. She's easy to be with when she's like this, so soft and tender.

'I'll have to go out for a while tomorrow.' I tell her. 'Don't change the locks while I'm gone, will you?'

She purses her lips and there's silence, then she grabs my hand and squeezes it. 'You will come home, though?'

I squeeze back. 'Of course I will. It's just for the day, mum, don't worry.' I kiss her head. 'And you never know, I might have some good news when I come back.'

She smiles up at me, the same sly smile from this morning. 'And I might too.'

I raise my eyebrows at her but she starts to unwrap herself from her blanket, face averted.

'Mum, what are you planning? You know I've never liked surprises.'

Sunlight rushes into the room through a break in the clouds and she blinks and turns. 'Oh, look, it's going to be a nice end to the day. Shall we go into the garden for a while? You can finish the weeding, like you promised.'

'You just keep coming with the treats, don't you?'

I help her into her wellies and coat and we go outside. I find the rake and continue my never-ending task of clearing the leaves while mum shuffles around the borders and flowerbeds, pinching off dead petals. She pauses at the far end of the garden and calls to me. 'Look how well your ferns are doing. Your grandmother used to pour the dregs of her afternoon tea on them every day to help them grow, but since you left home I've given them a pint of black coffee twice a week and they're thriving. Just look!'

I wander over. 'Well, they've certainly grown tall. They must like the caffeine.'

She bends to look at the wooden markers. 'That's the one we planted when you were born. Lady Fern. And that's the one your dad gave me to mark your fourth birthday. Hart's Tongue. And there's the Limestone Oak Fern. I tried a few others but none took like these. Aren't they magnificent?'

She's so pleased with herself that I can't bear to tell her the ferns are speckled with rot down by their roots, and though they may be tall there's something bedraggled and sickly looking about them. I watch her as she strokes the rustling fronds and picks off tiny flies. We could be any normal mother and daughter sharing an affectionate moment. For a second I waver on my plan to visit the great-aunt. Maybe I should just stay here instead, make more of an effort to be kind, to help her accept the loss of my father without resenting every moment she yearns for him. But then she steps back and looks up at me.

'You never did like these ferns, did you? Do you remember me catching you piddling on them when you were little? It was because your father planted them for you, wasn't it? You wanted to ruin any effort he made for you.'

I turn away and pick up the rake, reluctant to admit that,

yes, I always did hate the ferns, and yes, probably because of him. Definitely because of him. 'I was a child, for Christ's sake. Why do you always have to do that, pick at the scab? It's as if you only want me to remember the negative things about dad.'

Mum jerks back. 'What rubbish. I tried so hard to make sure you knew you were loved. It's not my fault that you took against him.'

'No, you didn't. You didn't try at all. You were jealous, mum, admit it. You didn't want to share him even with your own child. You still don't want to. All of my memories of him are bad ones, and that's down to you. But I've seen the photographs now. He loved me in those photographs, and I looked like I loved him.'

For a second I think she's going to contradict me, so embedded is her impulse to paint me as a child-demon, but then she looks stricken. 'Yes, you did love each other, and there were happy times, for all of us. I forget that sometimes.'

I'm not going to let her off the hook. 'You forget it because it doesn't fit with your view of the past and of what you had with dad, but that doesn't make it right.'

She mutters under her breath and we move away from each other, stiff-backed. I go inside to use the toilet and when I come out I can hear her talking downstairs. She's sitting at the kitchen table by the time I get to the hallway, wellies dangling from her feet, gazing at the cupboard with the gin in it.

'Who was that?' I ask as I go to the freezer for ice-cubes.

'Who was what?' She watches as I pluck a lemon from the bowl on the dresser and get her glass from the draining board. Her hands are clasped together in her lap.

'On the bloody phone, mum, who was on the phone?'

'Oh. Nobody. A salesman. Don't know why I answered it.'

I put her brimming glass in front of her and move to the fridge. Unease gathers like migraine behind my eyes, blurring the shelves. I can't see the peppers. I shut the door and move to the cupboard.

'Okay, beans on toast for dinner tonight. I can't be arsed to cook anything else. It'll be just like old times.' I smile at her and she gets the barb beneath the words, nods back at me.

She finishes her gin while I heat the beans. They taste a lot better than I remember.

A Pebble Shaped Like A Heart.

When you crouched to pick it up with a shout of delight, rubbed it on your trouser leg, I already had my hand held out. But you turned and presented it to our child instead, and my fingers fluttered like shot doves back down to my side. Neither of you noticed.

A pebble shaped like a heart. Sea-smooth and veined with delicate threads of quartz. I wanted it. I watched as our child turned it over and tapped at it, slid it into her pocket without a word of thanks. She looked over at me and caught my narrow-eyed gleam of jealousy, interpreted it as admonition and muttered a sullen, *thank you, daddy*.

We all turned again to our treasure hunt, peering into rock pools and weaving trails through the sand with our toes. Your bucket was half full of shells and stones and slivers of glass, mine virtually empty. The sun shone but the wind was cold and I wished I'd brought my cardigan. Our child tramped along in our wake, head wilting on her neck and scowling down at her sandals. Her hair was knotted around her cheeks. It needed a trim.

You stopped regularly to exclaim over some fresh find and I always paused to admire, raised my eyebrows at Fern to do the same. The way you let out a hearty yell each time you scooped up some cracked shell or twisted piece of driftwood made me want to clutch you close to my chest and shield you from catching sight of her scathing pout. You were trying too hard and she knew it.

I resolved to make more effort, to see treasure where you did and not just detritus, but I was too conscious of the sand gritting against the soles of my feet, the salt sting of the breeze. I wanted to go back to the car and declare this day officially over, return our child to her grandmother's keeping and spend the meagre time remaining to us alone with you. I wanted to sit down and have a tantrum.

The rain, when it came, brought smiles to all of our faces. I realised then that you had been as anxious as me to halt this failed attempt at Family. It no longer worked. So back to the car via the ice cream van and then home, with all of us singing songs. Even Fern was grinning through her raspberry sauce.

I tried to talk to you about it afterwards, rehearsing lies to blot the seeping pus of our child's dislike, but you wanted to kiss instead, and so we did.

She was still awake when I went up to bed that night. I ignored her as I undressed, tight-lipped and cool in the spotlight of her fret, but then I saw the heart-shaped pebble on my pillow. I cupped its perfect fit in my palm and carried it to the dressing table, and then I climbed into bed and wrapped my arms around her, whispering thanks into her neck. His gift to her and her gift to me.

Mine now.

7

I was eighteen when I broke into the school to steal the papers for my A level history examination. After a bottle of fizzy white wine on an empty stomach, it had seemed like such a good idea.

I'd received a couple of university offers from the mainland and though I was confident that I'd pass English literature and art, for history I needed a backup plan. And I'd made that promise to my mother that I was going to leave her and never look back. I reckoned I could do with a little extra help to keep that promise.

School-yard rumour had it that the headmaster kept the examination papers in the top drawer of the filing cabinet in his office, and rumour also had it that the caretaker was a drunk who forgot to lock up when he left for the night. I shook the last drops from the wine bottle into my mouth and hunted out my torch.

The window of the girl's toilets slid open easily beneath my hand, releasing tangy particles of bleach and body spray into my face and past me, floating invisible through the night. When I licked my lips my tongue furred with chemicals.

Two of the cubicle doors were shut and I shuffled by the window for a moment, staring, tensed against the sound of a flushing toilet that never came. I nudged the doors open with my foot, just to be sure, and let out a tiny scream when a pipe above the cistern hissed.

My reflection in the mirrors above the row of sinks almost made me scream again. My eyes were a fathomless black, flat and lifeless as tiddlywinks counters. All angles, all expression, all that made me *me* were distorted by the gloom and rendered grotesque by the hat that I'd taken from my mother's wardrobe and customised to suit my needs.

It was in crushed navy velvet, huge and floppy. I'd looped a pair of tights around my head a couple of times to keep it in place and it bulged monstrously above my eyebrows. The tights dangled from their knot below my ear. I looked as if I'd been garrotted.

For a moment I was fourteen again and terrified of this stranger in the mirror, but then the rest of the wine I'd drunk oozed into my bloodstream and I began to giggle. I folded at the waist, hands on my knees, and then down onto the floor. I could have sat there all night, rocking and snorting, but the lure of the headmaster's desk with its paper prize pulsed through my growing hysteria, sobering me and bringing me back to my feet. I eased open the door to the corridor and slipped through.

The moon in stripes across the noticeboards. Shadows thick as felt. I'd never known the school so empty, so quiet. There was something eerie about the stretched darkness that made me wish I'd started on that second bottle of wine instead of tucking it under my pillow for another evening.

At the far end the headmaster's office waited. All of the classroom doors were ajar, milky half-light sprawled across the desks. To stand or crawl? I settled on an awkward half-crouch, a stumbling zigzag along the length of the corridor that tugged the muscles in my thighs painfully. There were sweet wrappers on the floor below the lockers, splashes of crimson overlooked by a cleaner rushing through her tasks to get home to her family. I picked them up and pushed them into the pocket of my donkey jacket. Only another few yards now.

The town hall clock struck three booming notes and I jerked and careened into the wall. My left ankle twisted beneath me and something ripped, just above the tender ridge of scar tissue. I collapsed around it, marionette stiff, as the world tipped sideways and my vision blurred. Pain like a thousand tiny men in fluorescent jackets wielding a thousand tiny saws, all at the same time.

When I was finally able to raise my head the town hall clock was striking four and there was vomit all over my jacket sleeve. I was terrified that I'd done something awful to my ankle but I didn't want to look at it. All I wanted to do was rest my cheek on the floor and stay as still as possible until someone came to help. I wished I had a blanket to pull up to my chin and snuggle into. Was there one in my rucksack? I couldn't remember.

By the time the town clock had sounded five times I was in a sitting position, leant against the wall, and thirstier than I'd ever been. But I was nearer to the headmaster's office than to the water fountain by the lockers. I had to see this through. I tried shuffling on my bottom, left leg rigid before me, and then levered myself onto my good foot and hopped the last few steps.

The headmaster's office door was cool and slightly slimy against my forehead. Decades of greasy knuckles soaked into the grain of the wood. When I pulled back and focused, it gleamed in patches where my skin had stamped its own sweaty mark. There was a brass nameplate screwed on at waist height, and above that a dirty sheet of paper hung from a piece of sticky tape. The school rules. I had a quick re-read while I steadied my breathing. All earrings other than studs were banned, but it said nothing about stealing examination papers.

I gripped the handle and turned it. No movement. I tried again, pushing at the wood with my palm, swinging my hip into it. The caretaker must have been having a sober evening when he locked up. With something close to elation I swivelled round and limped back down the corridor, burying my face in the water fountain. I sucked in long, greedy gulps until my stomach sloshed with liquid. There was water all over the front of my coat and the brim of my hat was soaked through, spilling droplets down my neck so that I shivered with the delicious chill of it.

There was nothing more I could do. It was time to go home. Nearly six now, and two miles walk ahead of me. My arms throbbed as I hoisted myself into a kneeling position on the sill in the girl's toilets. A second's panic as my hat caught on the latch and was dragged off my head, but it swung from the knotted tights like a bonnet, taut across my throat and safe. I left the window wide open and headed over the playing field, no longer even trying to stay out of sight.

The sun was a blood orange resting on the distant hills, gathering its strength before making the final heave up into the sky. I walked home drenched in colour, peach and pink and auburn, a stained glass figure limping into the light.

Tommy drove past on his way to an early fare and he stopped and reversed back up the road until he was alongside me. His moustache glistened with morning tea. He asked if I was okay, probably thought I'd gone mad like my mother. I accepted a lift and travelled the last mile and a half in the back of his car, legs up on the brittle leather, head tipped back against the window so that I wouldn't lose sight of the sun's ascent. He dropped me at the garden gate and I bent and kissed his cheek, making us both blush. He stopped asking questions then, turned the radio up high and tipped his cigarette to me in farewell. I limped down the path and round to the back door.

There was plenty of ice in the freezer, mum always made sure of that. I folded a few cubes into a tea towel and sat at the table. The press of cold against my swollen foot made me sigh with pleasure.

Noises above me, and then mum opened the kitchen door and shuffled over to the window.

I thought I heard a car.

She stood for a moment, looking out, and then turned to the kettle, holding herself hunched and stiff. Another hangover. She tripped over my shoe and swore, kicked it across the floor and then looked at me properly.

What the hell are you wearing? Is that my hat?

I winced as I rolled the tea towel half way up my calf and then all the way down to my toes. The bones in my foot had disappeared beneath a shiny puffball of flesh.

I don't think I'm going to be able to make it in to school today, mum. I fell over and twisted my ankle, look. It's the bad one as well.

142

She bent to examine me and then groaned and clutched at her head, sinking backwards onto the floor between my knees. Her eyes shut for a moment and her lips twitched as she muttered silently, then she pushed herself up and bent over me once more.

We need to get you to the doctor's. I'll ring Tommy, and Alison at the surgery.

Her voice on the newly installed telephone was shrill with triumph and purpose. *Just see,* she seemed to be saying, *I told you I'd get a phone, and now just see how good a mother I can be, if only I'm given a chance!* She checked the clock on the wall and redialled, spoke to Tommy, nodded and checked the clock again. Then she replaced the receiver gently, still scared that it would break if handled too roughly, and bustled out of the room, calling over her shoulder for me to get ready, get out of that ridiculous outfit, hurry up and make myself decent.

As I travelled once more in the back of Tommy's cab on my way to the doctor's, catching his eye occasionally and smirking in embarrassed complicity, my night-time antics already felt like a distant memory or an anecdote told to me by someone else. I wondered what it was I'd wanted more: to cheat my way off the island or to get caught doing so. I hadn't planned any of it properly, hadn't made any attempt to cover my tracks. I had a horrible feeling I'd left my torch behind in the school corridor.

My head throbbed from the after effects of the cheap wine and I felt sick again. If this was how mum spent her every morning I had to admire her persistence in drinking every night.

I looked over at her. Her knuckles were white as she gripped the handbag resting on her knees. Every bump in the road induced a small groan of misery that had Tommy grimacing his concern. She turned her head and smiled grimly at me then faced front once more. Tiny droplets of sweat shimmered on her throat.

The sun reared from its place above the hills, now separated from land by a blue strip of nothing. I twisted to keep it in view as the road dived down into town but then it was lost behind the scented grey of the soap factory. The car edged through shadow and stopped alongside the doctor's surgery. I sat and ignored mum's impatience, the open door. I suddenly didn't want to get out. I didn't want to go anywhere. The future leered through the cab windows, a future unknown and away from here. It was too much. I wanted to take it all back; the university applications, the extra revision tutorials, the sneering at my mother's claustrophobic little routines and the safe boundaries of her neutered world. *Please just let me stay right where I am*. I had my answer. If I could repeat last night then I'd do it again with greater sabotage, ensure I was caught and any escape routes away from here closed to me for good.

My hands knotted around the headrest in front of me and I hung on, shaking my head, until Tommy took me gently by the arm and persuaded me out onto the pavement.

*

I'm joined on deck periodically by other passengers, share a half-smile and the bench for a while, but spend most of the ferry journey to Sorel alone. I've never been a good traveller, even car journeys can make me nauseas, but there's something about boats in particular that brings on a cold sweat almost immediately. Face stiff with salt spray and numb with cold, feet vibrating against the slow grind of the engines, I sit and try to work out whether the rhythmic flicker between my hipbones is morning sickness, seasickness, or even the confused tumbling of the baby itself, shifting and resettling with each rise of the waves. I'm too miserable to even raise my binoculars to peer at the morning mainland ferry as it passes us on its way to Spur.

When we dock I go below to fetch the car, negotiating my way around an amble of holidaymakers and day-trippers. The stench of diesel tips the balance of my queasiness just enough to make me gag and I drop my bag as I fumble my hands over my mouth. The spilled contents slither between blurred ankles and I have to scramble to retrieve everything safely. Nobody stops to help me.

I follow the signs to the town centre and then wind my way up a hill to the nursing home. It's in a beautiful spot, perched above the town and facing over the spill of rooftops to the sea. Before I go inside, I sit for a moment and stare out at the water. This is the island my granny grew up on, though I have no memories of her ever returning to visit. And now I know why. It's only an hour's ferry ride away and yet for her, with her self-imposed banishment, it could have been on the other side of the world. She'd loved it, according to her letters, had missed it like it was an animate thing, and had spent year after year standing on *our* island, gazing at it, imagining its streets and its fields, building it up in her memories and her fantasies until it became too great to ever be able to compete with reality. Like mum, she placed herself in a position where absence would lie at the heart of her life, and then she cradled it close. What is it about the women in our family that we do yearning so well?

I've brought the letters with me, though I'm not sure yet whether to show them to the great-aunt. If Granny Ivy had wanted her to have them then surely she would have posted them years ago, when they could have done some good for the pair of them?

I give my name to the uniformed lady at reception and wait while she speaks briefly into a phone. Then she waves me over and points down the corridor. 'Room five. It's just down there on the left. She's a bit,' lowered voice, 'tetchy today. She had a bad night. Enjoy your visit.'

When I knock there's no answer, so I hover for a moment and then knock again. Still nothing. I push the door open and step inside. The great-aunt is sat in one of those customised high armchairs, which seem specially designed to make old people look even older and smaller than they need to. Her feet dangle a few inches above the carpet and she stabs a button on the control pad resting in her lap with angry repetition.

'It's broken again. Look at this. Can you do anything with it?'

I take a look at the controls and press the downward arrow. The chair eases itself back to floor level. Embarrassed, she glares at me. 'Well, I could have done that.'

I bend to kiss her cheek and then sit beside her. I'm not sure how to start the conversation. Some jolly remark about the passing years or how little she's changed would just feel false, and probably sound false too. I try not to stare at her. She looks so much like Granny Ivy now, as Granny Ivy had looked in the last couple of years before she died. I realise with a guilty twitch that she, my granny, must have been so much frailer than my self-absorbed younger self had ever noticed. My memories of her are all gigantic and pulsing with energy.

The great-aunt stares back at me with less discretion. 'God, you look just like your mother. Do you remember, at Ivy's funeral, having to drag her off the sofa and up to bed? Drunk. Disgraceful.'

I nod and try to smile. 'Yes, like it was yesterday.'

She narrows her eyes. 'Still stings, does it? You've got to learn to let things go.'

The cheek of it, coming from her, jolts a snort from me. I try to turn it into a cough but she's sharper than I gave her credit for.

'Come on, out with it,' she barks. 'You're not here to be nice, you've obviously got something to say, so spit it out.'

'Why did you help me then, if you were so disgusted by mum's behaviour?' I ask. 'You could have walked away and left me to deal with her by myself.'

'I was going to,' she says. 'It wasn't my mess to clear up. But there was something disarming about you and your panic. For just a second there was a flash of him, your grandfather. I tried to find it again afterwards but it was gone, or maybe it was never there in the first place. That's probably nearer the truth. You're your grandmother through and through. Now, stop making small talk and get to the point.'

I'm relieved by her rudeness. From the moment I walked in here and saw her I knew I was angry with her. For abandoning me when I was young and grief stricken, and for excising her sister from her life as if she'd never been. I'd half believed what I'd said to mum about the importance of family and making amends while you still had the chance, but that was until I saw for myself just how prepared the great-aunt was to hang onto her bitterness.

At least this way we don't have to waste time and we don't have to pretend. I pull the wad of envelopes out of my bag and hold them out to her. 'I found these at mum's house. Granny Ivy wrote to you for years, letter after letter, but she didn't ever post any of them. I thought you might want to have them.'

She makes no move to take them. 'If she'd wanted me to have them then she would have sent them, wouldn't she? Don't interfere.'

I thrust the letters at her but she stays completely still with her hands resting in her lap, even when I lean over and place them on her knees. She doesn't break eye contact with me. 'I said I don't want them. Is that all you came for?'

'There was another letter, one you sent her. Saying you'd help her with something.'

She shifts her legs slightly, just enough to dislodge the envelopes and spill them to the floor. 'So?'

I sigh and try to warm my voice. 'So you must have written to each other at some point. I want to find my dad, that's all. Mum's not well and we want to know what happened to him. Granny Ivy might have mentioned something about him to you. She made a point of finding things out about people, digging down below the surface.' I wave a hand over the pile of envelopes on the carpet. 'These letters were full of him. She knew he was married even before my mum did.'

The great-aunt blinks for possibly the first time since I entered the room. 'So you've read the letters? You know what she did to me?'

'Yes, I know about her falling in love with my grandfather and running off with him. I know she was sorry.'

She laughs then. 'Not sorry enough to give him back. Not sorry enough to keep her hands to herself. I never loved anyone like I loved Edgar. Not even my poor husband. He tried his best but I was like ice. I think I froze him to death.

148

Did you know she used magic to steal him from me? And she was good at it, your lovely granny. He didn't stand a chance.'

I sit back in my chair and try to think of something to say which isn't reflexively defensive. Silence squats between us as I look around the room and she looks at me. I can't find inspiration in the biscuit coloured carpet or the white walls stretching blankly from corner to corner like faces turned away, expressionless. There are no books in here, no photographs, no ornaments. Nothing to take the chill off. I'd always imagined nursing homes as cosy places, room after room stuffed full of sentimental keepsakes and a lifetime of memories.

She knows what I'm thinking. 'What's the point of memories if they're all bad ones. I'm as content here as anywhere else.' And she does look content, almost cheerful as she stares me out and dares me to say anything to rock her from her moral high ground. She's just like the rest of them. The rest of us. Hanging tight to the absences in her life and using them to define her.

'At least she was happy with him,' I say. 'They lived their lives together and loved each other until he died. Whatever it was that brought them together in the first place, it lasted. And they had a child, and that child had a child.' I gesture to myself, as if it needed pointing out. 'And this child is having a child. Their love created so much.'

Her eyes almost close, then snap open again. 'How lovely for you all. And congratulations. But excuse me if I don't feel any joy for you. I loved Edgar as much as she did. I loved him more than I should have done.' She stresses the last words meaningfully. 'And when he left me, two weeks before our wedding, not only did he break my heart, he broke apart the baby I didn't even know I was carrying. His betrayal, *her* betrayal, ripped that baby clean from my womb. So there.'

Her triumph shocks me as much as what she's just said. Any pity I could feel withers before her jutted chin and clasped hands. I get up to leave, bend to scoop the letters from the carpet.

'Don't you want to know what we wrote to each other?' she asks. 'What we could possibly have to say? That's what you came for, after all. She asked me for a favour, one favour, and I granted it. Not for her, but for the names. For our family name, which still means something to me even if she was happy to drag it through the mud, and for his name, *your* name, because I loved him. I've still got the letter; you can have it if you like.'

I watch as she edges herself upright and walks with tiny, measured steps to a sideboard. So frail and old. Surely so lonely? But I'm guessing her bitterness keeps her warmer at night than any lover or friend ever could.

'Here.' She gives me a large padded envelope. 'It's in there. It should answer some questions for you, though don't come crying to me if you don't like what you read.'

I think about kissing her cheek again but can't bring myself to get that close. I nod instead, and float a hand in the air between us by way of goodbye. She's turned away before I open the door.

Back in the car I stroke the bulk of the envelope, pick at the seal. But I feel too shaky right now to open it. I'll wait until I get home.

Home. The thought lifts me. I want to see mum, spend a nice evening with her, play cards and bicker over the rules of rummy. She's got her faults, god knows she's got plenty of them, but at least she can still take some joy from life. Well, from gin and from squabbling with me anyway, and that's better than nothing.

There's a couple of hours wait for the next ferry home and I spend the time sat inside my car, heading the queue to board. When we're floating away from Sorel I release myself from its muggy confines and go up on deck. Stick figures line the dock, tiny Tonka Toy cars, and behind them all the faded mauve of heather on hillside. I stay leant against the rail for a while, watching the land slide away from me until it becomes just a smudge of charcoal beneath the clouds. My granny must have stood like this once, her hand clasped in my grandfather's, staring until her home shrank to nothing in front of her eyes. Was she laughing with the joy of having won over my grandfather, or was she crying at the necessary exchange of one love for another?

I turn away and totter to a bench, probably the very same bench that I sat on this morning, to endure the remainder of the journey. The sea is choppier now, throwing up handfuls of spray, and nobody joins me. I can see my island rising from the horizon and it anchors me.

Car alarms wail when I go below deck, electronic babies screaming their urgency until they're soothed by a return of attention. Everything has spilled from the parcel shelf of my car, map books in a jumble on the floor. I get in and start the engine, try to edge my way past the vehicles on either side so that I can be first off the ferry. I'm suddenly panicky, desperate to get home. I can't remember whether I told mum I'd put her lunch on a plate in the fridge. What if she tried to cook herself something one-handed or hunt down the gin while I was gone? I imagine her lying broken on the kitchen floor, calling out for help, and the image bullies me every inch of my ascent through the boat's belly.

Then I'm back outside and onto land again, past the shabby steel warehouses and through the gates. Tarmac fills the space in my rear view mirror, as if the day and the trip had only ever been an illusion. Nearly home now, and hopefully mum will have missed me a little as well, will be pleased to see me.

There's a strange car parked in my space by the garden gate, forcing me to move further up the narrow lane and deeper into the ditch where it's muddier. I'd be more irritated if I weren't so surprised. Mum's never had a visitor since I've been here. Through the net curtain, as I near the house, I can just make out two forms sitting close together in the lounge, framed by lamplight. Voices reach me as I open the front door and let myself in. Even though I recognise them both my brain won't assign a name to the visitor, and I'm still curious when I walk into the lounge.

Mum beams up at me and stretches out her hand. 'I thought I heard a noise. Look who's here.'

She's flushed with pleasure, giggling and smoothing at her hair. I turn slowly from her. My brain has finally caught up with my senses and I know who I'll see standing by the fireplace. Please god, may she not have told him.

Rick, when he steps forward and puts his arms around me, is shaking slightly. I only get a quick look at his face before mine is against his chest, but it's enough. He knows. She's told him.

A Tarnished Silver Chain

Tiny fish like dropped stitches of silver thread. It made us dizzy to look down at them, to look past our feet warm and poised on the stepping-stones, and so we'd throw out our arms and teeter and laugh, the three of us. You leading the way with fishing nets and buckets, our child safely sandwiched between us as she leapt from stone to stone and pointed everywhere. I carried our sandals and kept one hand stretched out to catch her should she fall, though she would only have splashed to the thighs in this river, scattered the silver fish and drenched her summer frock.

An afternoon sacrificed for Family. The two of us for once the three of us, and my face turned away to hide my bitten lip. I only turned back when I was sure I could smile at you both, and clap my hands, and say how pleased I was, what a good idea it was, and what fun we'd all have. But I think you knew, and you promised an evening alone very soon. Maybe even a whole night in our special place, just the two of us.

And so we sat or stood or squatted by the river, trailing nets through the icy gush, and I watched as my lover and our child held hands and whispered together. She frowned as she stared down into the wet, so desperate to catch something she could take home to her grandmother, and I saw you in that puzzled concentration. I laid out the rolls and the cake, passed around the thick glass bottles of forbidden fizz, scolded you both for dirtying your clothes and glowed as you exchanged glances and nudges. So this was what it would be like to be your only family, your proper family. The ones you came home to.

You were bending over her when the chain slipped from your neck, slithered across her arm and caught in her net. You hadn't seen it fall. I was at her side before she could speak and I scooped it out and held it in my fist, placed a hand on her shoulder and pressed lightly. She stared up at me with wide eyes, opened her mouth to speak, but then I pressed harder and she was silent.

I tucked the chain into the pocket of my dress and returned to the picnic blanket, continued with my exclamations, my fond commentary, playing wife and mother, reddened from the sun and the deceit. Our child had lost some of her glow but I put it down to too much sweetness and you agreed with me.

It was only much later, when she'd been put to bed and we were sat in your car in the lane outside the house, that you noticed the loss. It had been a gift, that chain, though from whom you'd never said and I'd never asked, but you were distraught. I stroked your arm and promised to return to the river to look, and when we kissed goodbye I licked its pattern from your throat and knew you'd miss me.

After you'd gone I went straight to my room and checked on our sleeping child. I opened my wooden keepsake box to make sure your chain was still there. I imagined the smell from that hollow between your collarbones trapped in its links.

I didn't dare clasp it around my own neck in case I forgot to take it off again, but it was enough just to have it.

8

I was nineteen when my mother finally realised that I wasn't going to contact her and began phoning me at university. It took her longer than I'd anticipated to get the hint.

I was studying in my room when the first call came through, eyelids heavy with glitter and Goethe. Two of my friends lay wrapped together on the bed, sleeping. I remember the knock on the door, the joyful leap up and away from my desk, the sudden dizzy tilt as last night's cider squeezed my brain a little harder.

I was still wearing my fancy dress costume, in love with the cobweb of chiffon around my legs and the stiff barrier of paint masking my face. No longer Fern. The boy, when I opened the door to him, leaned away for a moment, staring. I smiled at his confusion, at his eyes the rich brown of roasted almonds, and felt the paint crackling across my cheekbones. I hoped it wasn't starting to flake.

Okay, let me guess … Hell?

I shook my head and spun in a slow circle. The chiffon swooped and bristled around my calves, tiny threads sparking in the light. My wrist, as I raised it to lean against the doorframe, flamed with silk ribbon. Orange criss-crossed over red criss-crossed over purple. I bent my knee and twisted slightly at the waist so that the swell of hip would create a deeper curve and draw the eye.

Give up? I'm fire.

He nodded then, as if he'd been about to guess just that.

Well, Fire, there's a phone call for you. Your mother. She says it's urgent.

He didn't move away from the door. Behind me one of the sleepers snuffled and whimpered. I waited for him to ask what I was doing that evening, to suggest a drink at the union bar. In a green glass pot on my desk I stored my broken promises to unwritten essays and I willed him to speak so that I could add another. Soon the pot would be too small to contain them all and I'd have to get a bigger one.

When he did ask I pretended to think about it for a minute, watching him through a veil of thick, plum lashes. Then I laughed and twirled and he grinned his relief. Turned away and then, remembering, snapped his fingers and turned back.

Aren't you going to take that call? She sounded upset.

I walked with him down to the lobby and he pointed out his room, told me he'd meet me by the main entrance at seven. I stayed by the phone until he'd gone and then I picked the receiver up and floated it next to my ear for a moment, breath held, listening to the squawked confusion at the other end of the line. Then I pressed it gently into its cradle, waited for a moment to see if it would ring again, and danced back along the length of the lobby.

The warm, heavy bundle on the bed hadn't moved. I climbed onto the mattress and wedged myself into the soft dreams of my friends. Curled between the sweet damp of their breath, limbs flickering their descent into sleep, I sighed pleasure through crimson lips, trailing grease paint across the pillows. I hadn't realised that university would be this much fun.

By the next weekend she'd called five more times.

Fern, it's your mother again. She said it's important …
Hey, Fire, your mum's on the phone, what do you want me to tell her?
Phone call for you. I couldn't hear her properly, she sounded drunk, but I think it's your mum …
Your mother's on the phone again. Do you know what time it is? I've got an exam first thing tomorrow and she won't stop calling …

I wrote an instruction on a piece of card and impaled it into the wall above the phone, where nobody could miss it. *If Fern Gilbert's (Room 81) mother calls, please tell her that Fern is out. Thanks.* And when it began to feather at the edges, swinging crookedly from its pin, I wrote another. And then another.

Was that unnecessarily harsh of me? The young dress cruelty up as independence and excuse themselves for breaking their parents' hearts over and over, but for me it wasn't casual enough to be that. Because I wanted to hurt her.

157

I wanted her to know that I'd rejected her and the life she led. I'd made it off the island and I was never going back. I was young enough to believe it would be as easy as that.

Once or twice a month I'd scribble a few words on the back of a postcard.

All fine here. I'm studying hard. Hope you're well. Love F

Sometimes I'd even remember to pick it up from my desk on my way out to a lecture, drop it into my bag ready to take to the post box. And sometimes I remembered to dig it out of my bag before it became slimy with lip-gloss and sticky from humbug wrappers. But I rarely remembered to buy stamps from the student shop.

The not remembering became easier in the second year. Six of us sharing a house built for four. The garden our living room, blue tarpaulin stretched above the mossed patio slabs and mildewed armchairs. Bumblebees busy ransacking the buddleia that grew under the kitchen window. That was my happiest year. Not just of university, but ever. I loved to sit outside when it rained, curled in one of the armchairs, watching the sag of the tarp as it strained above me. The entire neighbourhood was given over to students, terrace after terrace fragrant with incense, my world a papier-mâché cocoon of lecture notes and dissertation deadlines.

There must have been times when it was cold, and we argued, and I was sick of people stealing my socks. I don't remember any of that, though. Like my mother with my father, and Granny Ivy with Sorel, my memory has skewed itself to fit my longings, and so I suppose it doesn't really matter whether any of it was actually true. It was the best year of my life because I remember it as the best year of my life.

The almond-eyed boy shared my bedroom for a while and then moved into the house next door. Essays were written on laps, ink stains glossing the cushions. Hair dye was applied at the kitchen table, tea towels muddy with henna. Childhood horror stories were swapped by candlelight when there weren't any spare coins to feed the meter. I was adopted. I was raised by an aunt who used to drink all day and beat me every evening. My father had died in a fire. He was a member of a rock band, I never found out which one, and my mother was a groupie who still dressed in leather and fishnets and hauled herself out, to god knows where, every Saturday night. I was a changeling, found wandering one morning by the woman I called mother, sparkling with dew and wearing nothing but two fern leaves in my hair.

I could be anybody I wanted to be.

It never occurred to me to tell the truth. Not once. I don't think I was ashamed so much as excited at the prospect of having a blank canvas spread before me, something that I could draw on, scribble over and embellish the corners of whenever I wanted. When you've lived your whole life on an island you have no concept of anonymity. Even with my family's unsociable tendencies I was known. My mother's unfortunate choice in lover was known. Her penchant for gin was known. But here I was Anybody. I even toyed with the idea of changing my name.

Shared suppers of pasta and peas. Coloured stickers guarding the milk cartons. Protest marches and movie hero posters. I was never alone. Friends of friends dropping round, talking until dawn, curled like kittens at the bottom of my mattress.

You don't mind if I get in with you, do you? I'm so cold, and your bed's the cleanest.

So many friends. They spilled over the garden wall, crawled out from under the kitchen table, leapt from cupboards. So many friends that I would trip over them in the morning, wading towards my first coffee through a carpet of flesh and blankets.

Sometimes I'd stop speaking mid-sentence, just to look around me at all the faces looking back. Sometimes I couldn't contain my love and I'd rush from person to person, fling fierce arms around them, whisper gratitude into their ear. And sometimes I'd tip my head back and search the sky for signs of a god, silently beg him to end the world right now. Because that moment, with the sun browning my feet and my friends layered around me so tightly packed that I couldn't see the ground, was as perfect a moment as I could wish for.

There were times when a drift of cherry blossom petals on a spring breeze would make me cry, though I couldn't explain why. The shout of the nesting rooks in the back garden would make me shudder and rush indoors. The smell of gin on someone's laughter would make me gag. At those times, just for a second, I'd forget who I was now. I'd stare into the sink and see amongst the dirty plates a mouth twisted with despair, swollen with tears. But then I'd turn the radio up and start to dance, and my friends would watch and clap, cheer me on until I spun myself into a heap across their laps and clung to them. The press of their bodies against mine grounding me once more. I'd left that other Fern behind on the day I left home, and I was never going back.

*

Standing in the garden in my new cherry red Doc Marten boots. My suitcase and two bin bags spilling from the boot of Tommy's car, my ferry ticket clenched between my teeth. I held her as she sobbed and squirmed, as she begged me not to go. All I wanted to do was spit the thin cardboard onto the ground and stamp it into the dirt, drag my things out of Tommy's car and shut myself into the echoing, empty space that used to be my room. Couldn't she see how scared I was? Why did she have to make it so much worse for both of us?

The hot trickle of her tears against my collarbone, the frantic scratch of her nails on my arms, the vibration of her sobs deep inside my rib cage, and behind her the look of pity and anguish on Tommy's face. He nodded at me, tried to pull her away, and she flailed against him, smearing her grief across his shirt in shining trails. She turned and ran inside the house.

I got into the car. Still time for her to splash her face with water, to blow her nose and come back outside to wave me off. Still time for her to make this right. Tommy lit a cigarette and fiddled with the radio. Switched the engine on and eased the car into gear, back into neutral. He adjusted the rear view mirror, sighed and shook his head.

What do you want to do, love?

The window in the living room slapped shut. The yellowed curtain glided across to fill the pane. My mother had made her decision.

I tugged the ferry ticket from my mouth, tearing the skin from my lip, tasting blood.

Let's go.

And as the car bumped down the lane to join the main road, the sudden breath I released was thick and dark with relief. I had a ferry to catch.

I didn't look back.

*

We watch each other as we sit around the table and eat dinner. Every time I catch mum's eye she smiles and nods at me. *Didn't I do well?* She's taking gleeful advantage of Rick's presence and her own sense of achievement, gulping gin between mouthfuls of chilli, nudging the glass back to me for refills.

The conversation stutters and stalls, stumbles on. I insert garlic bread into the silences, keep my hands clenched around the desire to reach across and throttle my mother. The meddling bitch has managed to screw up my life without even having left her own front room. I just can't work out how she did it. My heart has been spurting acid and adrenaline since I got home and the muscles in my calves keep twitching. He was probably on the mainland ferry that passed me this morning, the one time I didn't use my binoculars to check for him, and now he's here, in this house, and he knows my secret. I stare at him when his gaze is fastened to his plate, glance quickly away when his chin tips back up. Mum chuckles fondly as I revolve around the room yet again and points with her spoon.

'Come and sit down, Fern, and finish your food. She's been like this ever since she got here, Rick, but I was the same when I was pregnant with her. Couldn't sit still for five minutes.'

Rick flinches and spears his fork into his lip. Blood wells instantly, thick droplets trembling down onto his mound of rice. Can't she see the effect that word is having on him? How many times has she mentioned my pregnancy in the last hour? It's got to be deliberate. I glare at her and she beams back at me with hazy affection. Rick grimaces and stirs the pink grains into the sauce while I jump up again to tear some pieces of kitchen roll. As I pass them to him across the table he takes my hand and won't let go. Another trickle, a perfect bloody teardrop, oozes down his chin and drips onto his plate but he doesn't try to wipe it away, just holds tight to my fingers and stares up at me. Mum chatters on, peering around my body to get his attention.

'Trying to get hold of you for ages he was, but you see, Rick, I never usually answer the phone. It's always a cold caller or a wrong number, isn't it? I didn't spoil the surprise, did I, Fern? You didn't guess what we were planning?'

I prise the crumpled wad of kitchen roll from Rick's fist and gently press it to his lip, wincing apologetically down at him. 'No, mum, you didn't spoil the surprise.'

She tries to pat my arm and knocks her glass into the salad bowl. 'You'd better get me another one of those, love. And what about some ice cream? Rick, would you like some ice cream?' Speaking too loudly now, over-stressing each syllable. I feel a brief embarrassment for her, a pinch of protectiveness. But a glance at Rick shows me that he's still too immersed in his own shock to really take in mum's undignified state.

I start to collect the plates, run water into the sink. Rick moves to stand next to me. 'Let me help you with that.' I don't look at him, just take what he passes me and stack it on the sideboard. Mum stays hunched at the table, elbows splayed and speckled with rice, waiting for me to turn around so that she can repeat her request. The water's too hot but I plunge my hands in anyway, taking grim pleasure from the sting of it.

'Fern? Are we going to have another drink? Fern?' Mum's voice has become a whine. The evening's triumph is slipping away from her and she doesn't understand why I'm not being more attentive. 'Can't we have some ice cream and another drink, Fern?'

Rick glances at me and then puts the tea towel down and turns to her. 'I'll get it for you, Iris. Where do you keep your bowls?'

'Oh, just get me that drink if you would, Rick, and don't worry about the ice cream. I've got to watch what I eat; I've got a dodgy heart you know.'

I snort and launch plates into the sink, food still attached. Bits of green pepper swirl and subside below the brown foam like diving frogs at a muddy pool. My hands are swollen now, blotched and crimson. I float them on the waves I've created, fingers spread wide over the oily film suffocating the water, and stare into the murk. My heart is throbbing inside my eardrums and I don't respond to the knock on the door until it repeats and Rick turns from the dresser, juggling glass and lemon. 'Do you want me to answer that?' I shake my head and walk out of the kitchen.

Tommy stands on the step and smiles tiredly at me. 'Hello, love, I popped round earlier and your mum told me you'd gone visiting. Can I have a word?'

I try to edge outside and pull the front door closed behind me but mum's already thrust her chair back. 'Is that Tommy? Come in and meet Rick.'

We just look at each other, neither of us moving, until mum appears at my side and tugs us into the hallway. She's delighted at this interruption, this chance to recapture her self-satisfaction and tell again how she managed to arrange such a wonderful surprise for her daughter. Tommy murmurs, 'I need a word with you, Fern,' as he passes me. I think about just walking out, leaving them all to it, but I follow him into the kitchen.

Rick's already shaking hands with Tommy when I remember and I rush forward and try to catch his eye, either of their eyes, to stop the exchange that must surely follow. Too late.

Rick glances at me. 'Tommy? Fern's dad? I thought you'd… Fern told me that you'd gone. That's why she's here. Isn't it?'

I sit at the table and watch his frown of confusion, watch it mirrored on Tommy's face and then on my mother's. I press my hands to my blush.

'I'm not Fern's dad,' and 'He's not Fern's dad,' both spoken at the same time. Then Rick again. 'Yes, you are. Aren't you? Fern always talks about you. I was sorry to hear about you and Iris splitting up.'

They all look at me but I don't raise my gaze from the table top. 'I said he was *like* a dad to me,' I tell the pepper grinder.

Rick shakes his head with exaggerated emphasis. 'No you didn't. You said he was your dad. You said it more than once.'

The silence that follows is excruciating. I bend my head and wrap my hands around the goosebumps that are prickling across the nape of neck. There's no way I can deflect this, or even laugh it off. Mum and Tommy are just confused but I don't need to look at Rick to know that he's not going to back down to spare my embarrassment. He can't express his public shock at one example of my deceit so he'll make damn sure he has the opportunity to express it at another. All I can do is come clean.

I look up at Tommy. 'Yes, I'm sorry, I did say you were my dad.' I shrug and stand. 'I've always wanted you to be. I've always hoped there might be a chance. You and mum…'

He gives mum a quick look then, no more than a flicker of pupil, but she reddens and retreats behind outrage. 'How could you, Fern? Lying about your own father. I'm so ashamed, I can't tell you how much.' She snatches her glass and leaves the room at a near run.

Tommy, redder even than her, but gentler, strokes my arm. 'I'd love to be your dad, Fern, and I'm touched that you'd say I am, but if you know it can't be true you shouldn't lie. Your poor young man here doesn't know what to think.'

I glance at Rick and then refocus on Tommy. 'I know. I'm sorry. But there was something though, between you? It might not be impossible?'

'No, love. There's no chance. Whatever may have been between Iris and me, and I'm not saying there ever was, you aren't a part of it. Just let it go.' He steps away and nods at Rick. 'Sorry about all this. It was nice meeting you anyway. Fern, will you walk out with me?'

We're silent until we reach the garden gate. I'm in no hurry to go back inside, am content to lean beside him and stare at the house. The twin silhouettes of mum and Rick occupy different windows, both looking out at us. I wonder what they're thinking, as they strain through the twilight. Are they still angry with me? Such different reasons for their anger, but both justified.

Tommy fishes his car keys out of his trouser pocket and fidgets with them. 'You went to see Ivy's sister today, then? How did it go?'

The question makes me remember how he drove away from me up at the viewing point the other day. How he didn't want anything to do with helping me look for my father. I tell him as much, though with less conviction than I would have had previous to him finding out about me adopting him as a parent. He has the grace not to bring that up, but pursues the question more urgently when I straighten to go back in.

'Fern, wait. What happened with her? Did she tell you

anything? I wouldn't listen to a word that woman says, you know. Your grandmother said she was born a meddler.'

Rick's form disappears from the window, and a second later so does mum's. Are they united in the hall, talking about me? But then light pools on the step as the front door opens. Rick calls my name and I move towards him. 'I'm here, just saying goodbye to Tommy.'

He stays where he is, just outside the door, and I kiss Tommy's cheek quickly. 'I'd better go. I've got some explaining to do.'

'Fern, did she tell you anything?'

I stare at him. 'Why do you want to know? She gave me a couple of things. A letter and something else. I haven't had a chance to look at them yet.'

Rick clears his throat and I turn to the sound. 'I've got to go, Tommy. Thanks for coming by and I am sorry for the mix up earlier.' I grimace at him, hoping to raise a smile.

He shakes his head. 'Maybe you shouldn't look at them, love. Just bin them, or give them to me. Maybe it's for the best.'

'What do you mean? Do you know something?' I take his arm and put my face close to his to peer at his expression, but then Rick says my name again and I hear his footsteps on the gravel behind me. He has my coat over his arm and drapes it around me as Tommy shuffles for a moment and then gets slowly into his car. I raise a hand in farewell as he drives away.

Rick and I walk around the house to the back garden, our breath plaiting the air in front of us, and I lean into him. All I want now is to be able to fast forward the next couple of hours and have him forgive me, have him lie beside me in my childhood bed. He stops us under the oak, wrists resting on my shoulders. I smile into his solemn expression, trying to buy a little time.

'You've got more white hairs.' I stroke the side of his face. 'There was a time when I could count each individual one and now there's so many. How did I not notice before?'

'When were you planning to tell me?'

So we're going to do this right now, with mum no doubt leaning from the living room window so as not to miss a word. I sigh and drop my hand to my side, try not to sound sullen. 'I don't know. Tomorrow. The day after. Does it matter? You know now.'

His voice rises, making me jump. 'Of course it matters. You're having my baby. That's why you went in such a hurry, isn't it, because you found out? It clearly wasn't because your dad had left and your mum needed you. That's if she's even your mother.'

I suddenly realise how hurt he is. How angry. And my own anger rolls over inside my chest, stretches and sharpens its claws. Yes, let us do this now.

'Mum did need me. I couldn't just leave her to cope by herself.'

The years of doing just that, of not returning calls, of leaving her to cope, fan out on the ground between us and I trail into silence. He knows enough about my life and my relationship with her to know that I'm lying. He probably knew I was lying at the time but just didn't know why.

I think of the last night we were together, before I came here. The piles of clothes and shoes heaped over the bed, draped over the sofa. Me charging around the flat, dragging a suitcase, moving, constantly moving. Staying a few steps ahead of him throughout the evening, squeezing myself past his hugs and slipping out from his kisses. There was nowhere

168

for him to sit down. I chattered my concern for my mum, spilling words over my shoulder, never allowing him space to question me, and by the time we'd said goodbye I'd almost forgotten myself why I was really leaving.

The oak tree drips shadow from its branches, making crazy paving of Rick's face. He doesn't speak. I start to fidget. I want to salvage something from this before it's too late.

'How long can you stay for? It is lovely to see you, I hadn't realised how much I'd missed you. Shall we go to bed and talk about the other things in the morning?' I reach again to touch his cheek and move towards him but he shifts away, holding me at arm's length.

'We need to talk about this now, Fern. What are we going to do? I can stay for a few days, give us a chance to sort something out. Shit, I just can't believe you didn't tell me.'

Now I move away. 'Sort something out? What do you mean by that?' Outrage wraps itself around me, a suit of armour all spikes and sharp edges, and it's wonderful. I don't let him answer.

'I didn't ask you to come here, and I didn't ask you to share this baby with me. She's mine. There's nothing to *sort out*. Christ, Rick, when have I ever put pressure on you to do anything but love me?'

'I didn't mean *that*...'

I try to take a breath, slow myself down before I say anything else, because anything else I say is going to be needless and cruel. But the anger feels so much better than the guilt.

'And how dare you sneak around behind my back, scheming with my own mother to ambush me.'

Slow down. Take another breath. Don't say anything else. Not right now, when you're feeling cornered. Just look at him and remember why you love him. Please don't ruin this.

But I can't stop. 'And if you think you can just turn up here and start issuing orders, decide what's best for me and my baby...'

Above our heads the oak trembles loose a desiccated leaf. It spins on the breeze, trailing decay, and catches in my hair. Rick disentangles it, crumbles it between his palms and pulls me close. His hands are powdery against the nape of my neck.

'Don't, Fern. Don't shut me out again. I do want this baby, of course I do.' He kisses my closed eyes. 'But you're going to have to start being more honest with me.'

I'd wrestled the suit of armour off, prepared to let it drop to the ground beside me, but now I heave it back on, and tighter than ever. I make no effort to keep my voice low. 'What's that supposed to mean?'

He tries to keep his hands on me but I shrug him away and step back. 'Well?' I demand.

'You know exactly what I mean. This. You tell me that you've barely spoken to your mother for years but then you find out you're pregnant and you take off at a run and hide behind her. You close the door on me. You tell me all about your lovely dad and then I find out he's not your dad at all. Come on, Fern, you know exactly what I mean.'

'So you're calling me a liar, that's what you're saying, that I'm nothing but a liar.'

He spreads his arms helplessly. I watch him for a moment and then turn and start to walk back to the house. 'I think you should leave. I don't want you here.'

Tears are already filling the dark crevice behind my eyes. My cheekbones feel puffy with the effort not to let them fall, pressure bowing the spaghetti-brittle bones that cage my brain until I think they're going to crack open and spill their contents. I concentrate on the small crunch-crunch of my footsteps across the grass, concentrate entirely on the sound so that I can't hear Rick speaking behind me and I don't turn back.

Mum must have caught at least part of our argument because she calls out to me as soon as I'm in the hallway. 'Fern, is that you? Is everything okay?'

His coat dangles from the newel post. His car keys are on the dresser. I turn around slowly. No sign of a bag. I'm outside again and he's standing in the lane, face rendered grey by moonlight. He starts to say something as I hand him his keys and the tears almost come then but I don't let them. I press my hands to my eyes to keep them from swelling out of their sockets and springing loose like a couple of ghoulish jack in the boxes.

He gets in his car and starts the engine. 'I'll find somewhere to stay for the night. I won't leave the island until I've spoken to you.' And then he drives away.

A bend in the lane and he's gone. Too late to run after him. Too late to call him back.

Mum's waiting at the front door. 'What's going on? Where's Rick?' She follows me inside. I empty the sink and refill it, testing the water until it's slightly hotter than I can bear. I start to wash the plates and she grabs the tea towel and stands beside me.

'What did you do, Fern? You sent him away, didn't you? He was a lovely man and you ruined it for yourself, just like you used to ruin all your nice things when you were little.'

I can cry now if I want to. Or I can shout at mum, blame her for everything that's ever gone wrong with my life, for the mistakes that are hers, which I seem destined to repeat. I slide to the floor and let the tears come.

'He's gone, mum. I don't know why I did it but I couldn't stop myself, and now he's gone.'

She squats beside me with a grunt and puts her good arm around me. 'Then get him back, love. Tell him you're sorry. You can do that if you let yourself. You've got the baby to think of now. I didn't have a choice with your father but you do.'

A tendril of her hair brushes against my mouth and when I take a breath in it slips inside, feathering my tongue, choking me. I try to push her away but she clings on.

'Don't, Fern.'

I can barely speak for sobbing. 'But I'm just like you, mum. I tried so hard to be different, I hated the way you lived, but I'm just like you.'

She rocks me gently, rubbing my back. 'No, you're nothing like me, love, don't be so stubborn. Just say you're sorry and everything will be okay.'

I pull away slightly and look at her. 'He's married, mum. I *am* just like you. I've done exactly what you did.' Then I lower my head back to rest on my knees.

Above me, she rocks and mutters.

A Creased Page From A Map Book, With A Wooded Area Ringed In Red

Our shadows stretched grotesque beside us. We were a misshapen monster with four arms, four legs, writhing in agony. Collapsed down and ripped apart to create two human forms, and then coupled again as one monstrous beast. I liked to keep my eyes open and watch you glide and swoop above me, arch and twist below me, or else turn my head to the side and watch our shadow creatures wrestle.

Are they still there, I wonder? Our favourite place, moss soft and honeysuckle sweet, and our shadows locked forever in silent passion. I've never been back but I like to imagine them there, even now when the sun's shuttered by cloud.

And is it still the same? Or is it now a children's playground? A concrete walkway? A private garden? Do people sit where we used to lay and arc sandwiches through the centre of our ghost-selves, dragging parts of our past into their mouths with each intake of air? Do they scatter cool drops of water over the dim kick of my shadow-legs?

Our favourite place. Sorel. The furthest you ever took me from home, a ferry ride away, another island. Similar but not the same. Sorel. I loved the way it sounded in my mouth. I'd whisper it when you were gone from me, turn away from my mother's flinch and close my eyes. Plunder my memories until my kneecaps melted down my shins and I had to leave the room. Sorel.

Walking up the gangway onto the ferry, clutching camera and basket and each other's hand. Trying so hard not to look at you or I'd rush too soon in my mind to our place, to what we'd do there, and strangers would see it on my face. Walking away from the ferry and out to the growl of waiting taxis, a few inches of space between us on the back seat, intercepted glances, tightened fingers, tightened breath.

A picnic in a wooded valley, two tourists enjoying the sun. A generous tip and a pause to wave and watch until he was gone, and then we'd dive into the undergrowth, trample bluebells, part trails of ivy until we arrived at our secret place. Our favourite place.

You undressed me slowly, circled me as I stood and waited. You pulled me down onto the moss and we didn't undress at all. You lay at my feet and I stepped around you, over you, shedding clothes piece by piece.

We stayed for hours and murmured fairy tales into each other's stomachs. We gave the taxi driver instructions to wait on the roadside. We stayed the whole night and tried to light a campfire, shivered through the pre-dawn chill.

I always cried a little when we left, and pretended I had an allergy to the ivy, and you always believed me, or said you did.

How often did we go there? How many times in all? Thirty? Forty? Surely that's enough to imprint our reflections on the thick forest air, the spongy forest earth. Surely that's enough to leave a trace of what we had and what we did.

I never speak its name now. Sorel. And if I hear it I flinch as my mother used to, but then I think of our shadows still lying there, still clasped, and I can't help but smile.

9

I was twenty-one when I collapsed beneath an accumulation of dissertation deadlines and revision notes. I hadn't realised that paper could weigh so much. First a tremble started in the tendons around my ankles. Within a week it had skittered up past my calves. It was as if someone were tickling me lightly with a palm full of brambles. Then a quiver rippled out from the soft meat tucked inside my kneecaps and they tap-tapped their own rhythm when I walked.

Within a fortnight I was shaking so much I needed to use both hands to light a cigarette. I couldn't grip a pen. Hours spent locked in my room with the *Family Medical Encyclopaedia*, furtively looking up diseases, convinced I had something terribly wrong with my nervous system. Convinced I was going to die.

My friends stayed awake with me through night after night, holding my hand and spoon-feeding me cornflakes. They searched the house and found the yellow slips for tardy attendance I'd stockpiled over the months, and they met with my lecturers to beg for essay extensions. I kept the curtains closed and stayed in bed every day until teatime, floating like litter across my bed sheets. In the evening they'd persuade me downstairs to study with them at the kitchen table, box me in with textbooks and quote passages from Browning and Keats. Hands fisted against my cheeks, poetry smirched like soot across my vision, I'd scream and sweep the books from the table.

I can't do this! I can't!

Finally they made an appointment for me at the student health centre and frog-marched me there when I refused to leave the house. Flanked by bodies on either side, pummelled by a spring sun at my back, I flinched forwards on divining-rod legs. Cracks in the pavement loomed like caves that I could creep inside but I wasn't allowed to slow my pace.

Come on, Fern, you can't stop now. This isn't fair on us either, you know. We've all got our finals in a few weeks.

I spat reproach at them as they hustled me through the doors and handed me over to a nurse. I wilted as I watched them walk away from me. Their smiles were pink and plump with relief as they turned to wave goodbye.

The nurse led me into a side room and took my blood pressure. It was only when she hushed me, hands gentle on the sides of my face, that I realised I'd been doubled over in the chair, hair brushing the carpet, making that high-pitched sound my mother used to. And that's when the reality of what I'd let happen, of how much damage I'd done to my future, really hit me.

The nurse helped me undress and tucked me into a hard,

high bed. She told me to rest. The blinds at the window slatted the sunlight so that it cut sharp strips of shadow into the walls. I closed my eyes and started to drift. The smell of antiseptic. Low voices in another room. My left ankle began to throb and the shaking in my limbs settled and then stilled. It was going to be okay, I was only seventeen. It was all still ahead of me. I hadn't ruined anything, not yet.

When I opened my eyes the wall was all shadow and I was twenty-one again. A different nurse stood by my bed, leafing through a cardboard file that had my name inked on the cover. She smiled down at me.

Well, we've spoken to your mother and let her know where you are. She's very worried about you. When was the last time you ate a proper meal?

She brought me a glass of milk and a couple of neat, white tablets on a tray, then pulled up a chair and sat by me for a while. She knew about the crow chasing and the balancing rituals and she thought she understood me.

You're not the first, you know. Lots of our more fragile students suffer a breakdown when it comes to their finals. The pressure can get too much.

She used her words like White Spirit, scraping layers from the glossy new skin I'd painted myself with over the last three years, scrubbing at stubborn patches until the old skin re-emerged, wincing and raw. The new Fern, so carefully constructed, and so quickly stripped away.

I lay and watched the sun cast its lemon rectangles around and around the room as arrangements were made to send me home. I signed papers and offered excuses for why mum couldn't travel to collect me. My clothes were brought in by my friends and folded on a chair by the bed, but the effort it would have cost me to get up and dress myself was too much. I needed to channel all of my energy into relinquishing the me who might have been. Inside me, a parade of tablets fizzed and emptied their contents into my bloodstream at regular intervals, keeping me remote and sleepy.

Maybe I could have fought the process, insisted that I was well enough to sit my finals. Maybe I should have. But the nurse had been wrong; it wasn't the prospect of the exams that had shattered me, it was the prospect of the world beyond them. For those years at university really were the best years of my life and so I'd begun grieving for them before I'd even lost them.

All of my friends came to visit, pockets stuffed with promises to never lose touch. I nodded and hugged, gazed over their shoulders or down at the floor so that they wouldn't see into my eyes and frown their confusion. *You're not Fern. Where is she?* They surrounded me, balanced on the balls of their feet, ready to sprint into their futures. I wanted to grab their wrists and pull them down to their knees beside me, force them to fail in their dreams so that they would stay with me and live mine. *We could do it all again. Stay just as we are and re-sit next year.* But I didn't speak. I was colder than I needed to be when they said goodbye.

An escort drove me to the train station and found me a seat. I saw him speaking to a guard on the platform, the shared glance towards my window. I'd be plagued by curiosity disguised as concern throughout the journey home now.

The landscape segued from grey to brown to green. The occasional ruddy blotch of deer feeding in the fields. I tucked my feet up onto the seat opposite and chain-smoked as I watched it all flow past the glass. My muscles were stiffened against the first jolt of the truly familiar. Only then would I be able to accept that this was happening to me, that I really was going home, returned to my past like an unwanted package.

But when it came I had my eyes shut, half-dozing, and I wasn't prepared. The smell of the sea. It grasped my ankle and pulled me down so that I spluttered and thrashed in my seat. Then upright once more, nose against the window. I couldn't see it, not yet, but it saturated my senses.

The ferry crossing was quicker than I remembered, the ferry shinier and louder. I stayed below deck, squinting through cigarette smoke, so that I wouldn't have to see the mainland slipping away from me and Spur looming towards me. I didn't think I'd be able to bear seeing that.

Tommy was waiting in the car park at the dock, vast and still amongst the ebb and flow of the crowds. The hair tufting from under his cap was thinner and greyer and his face was a web of wrinkles. I stopped in front of him and sagged, tears blurring my first proper sight of home. He patted the air above my shoulder delicately and bent to take my case.

It's good to see you, love. Where's the rest of it?

I'd left behind everything that had belonged to the other Fern. I didn't need it anymore. I shrugged and walked ahead of him to his car in my cracked and faded, cherry red Doc Martens, and focused on the loose slap-slap of worn soles against tarmac. He tried to talk on the journey home, awkward attempts at conversation that I didn't respond to.

Mum was fidgeting at the open front door when the car

stopped by the garden gate. She rushed to me, arms spread, stumbling down the uneven path in her slippers. She'd put on weight, jiggles of fat frolicking around her jaw and stomach. Behind me, I could sense Tommy averting his eyes.

And then I was squeezed against her.

Oh, Fern, it's so wonderful to have you home. You've dyed your hair red! Come inside, darling, and rest. We'll soon have you right as rain.

I turned to thank Tommy as she led me away and he nodded and got back into his car. My mother hadn't even noticed him standing there. She chattered as she shut me into the house.

Well, it's very bright isn't it, and I think I preferred it brown, but it does suit you. I've made you an appointment with Dr Harris, he knows all about what happened. You mustn't worry that I'm disappointed, it was just all too much for you. But you're home now. You're safe. Oh, Fern, apart from the hair you look just the same, you haven't changed at all.

She unpacked my case and examined my blister packs of tablets while I sat at the kitchen table and looked around the room. The kettle was different. The dresser stood bowed beneath the weight of half a dozen bottles of wine and gin. Everything had a blur of grime. I was home.

I pushed myself to my feet and walked through the hall and up the stairs to my old room. The bed was covered with a new duvet and pillows. The curtains were drawn. I lay down and faced the wall and when mum came in a few minutes later I closed my eyes. The floorboards creaked as she shifted in the doorway for a moment and then left.

I kept my eyes closed and concentrated all of my energy on willing my hair to grow. The sooner the original brown swallowed that alien red, the sooner I could forget that I had ever been anyone else but the person lying in this bed right now. It was over. I should never have believed I could get away.

*

Mum keeps seeking me out to talk about Rick, to marvel at the similarities between us. She's gloating just a little and I can't really blame her. The years of my condemnation, my refusal to pity her or understand the love that prompted her to sell herself so short, lie unspoken between us and I'm just grateful that she's only gloating a little. I've stopped crying now but she hovers over me and trails tissues from her sleeve in a never-ending stream of apricot, just in case I need them.

He said he'd call. He said he wouldn't leave until we'd spoken. But the phone doesn't ring. I've checked it twice already this morning and had to pretend I was just giving it a polish with my jumper sleeve when mum appeared at my shoulder with a knowing smile.

I sat by myself in the kitchen last night after she'd gone to bed and remembered the sting of Rick's stubble-scrape across my chin, the protuberant bone in his big toe that reduces him to a hobble if he walks too far. I rehearsed words to bring him back or drive him away altogether, swinging between outrage that he could call me a liar and shame that I've lied to him so much. I tried writing things down as they occurred to me, scribbling and crossing through, muttering to myself until I suddenly realised what I would look like if another person entered the room. Then I rushed upstairs, stooped to stand before the mirror in my room, searching myself for my mother but finding only me.

I wonder if there was always something deliberate about my choice of lover and lifestyle, a subconscious need to get closer to mum by copying her, trying out her life the way I used to try on her heels when I was a child.

'How did you do it?' I ask mum over lunch. 'Year after year, never knowing when he'd come for you. Weren't there times when you just wanted to end it, give yourself a chance with someone who'd be free to love you back?'

She ponders that as she strokes her hair away from her face. It's nearly all grey now but it suits her. 'Of course there were, but those times didn't come often enough. I adored your father but I think I also adored the situation itself in a strange way. It appealed to me.'

I think I hear a car in the lane outside so I get up to check. As I take my seat again, stooped with disappointment, I avoid mum's eye.

'How did it appeal to you?' I ask. 'Was it the excitement of sneaking around and being the other woman?'

She moves her head minutely and is silent for so long that I think she must have forgotten the question. But then she sniffs and starts to speak.

'When I met your dad I didn't know he was married but he was always so mysterious, so elusive, his wife might as well have been standing behind him every time we were together. Then I found out about her and it was as if I'd been handed a gift. I was suddenly freed from the conventional fairy tale trappings, the worrying about whether he'd ask me to marry him, whether he'd still love me as much after we'd shared a bed and a routine. It's the way for us Gilbert women. Your grandmother was the same, wasn't she? You know about her and my father.'

She reaches for her glass while I stare at her. 'The letters? You've read them?'

'Of course I have. I was determined to find something that would explain my mum and dad, and what they had. You forget, Fern, I grew up in a house with two people who loved each other fiercely and exclusively. I could see from a young age they weren't like other parents.' She chooses not to see my raised eyebrow. 'Sometimes your granny would smile at him and his breath would leave his chest in one big rush as if she'd put her mouth against his and sucked it out. And she never stopped having that effect on him. When I found the letters that's when it all made sense; it was stolen love, and sinful, and that's why it was so special.'

I don't know what to say. So her view of love is based on a belief that the best kind is the one that you haven't any right to. Stolen love. She watched her parents and drew that conclusion even before she found the evidence to back it up. And have I in turn based my view of love on hers? It makes me shiver a little, to think of how far-reaching the collapsing dominoes of fate and learning are. If I were to research the family tree a little further, would I find an adulterous affair buried in my great grandmother's past? Would I hand this legacy down to my own child?

Mum pushes her plate away and gets to her feet. 'He will call you, Fern. Don't worry yourself about that. I'm going to try and have a nap now but come and get me if you need me.'

She strokes my hair on her way past. I catch hold of her hand to stay her. 'But would you do it again? You've got the advantage of hindsight now, and the loneliness of the last twenty years. Surely you wouldn't do it again?'

Her eyes fill with tears. 'Again and again and again. I love him. But the real question is: would I want that for you?

Because, no, Fern, I wouldn't. It hurts me to think of you going through any of what I've been through. It may have suited me but you're a very different creature. Despite the similarities, despite the child you're going to have.' She shakes her head and shifts slightly so that she can look at me.

'If he'd met me first he'd have married me, I know it, and maybe he'd even be sat in this room with us right now. But I've thought about it a lot over the years and I've come to the conclusion that I wouldn't have had it any other way. If he'd met me when he was free to marry me I might not even have loved him enough, not without the sinful baggage. And then there wouldn't have been you.'

She shrugs and laughs, and tugs her hand loose. I let her go. I can't remember ever being with her like this, so close, and I'm suddenly keen to end the moment now, before one of us says the wrong thing and the other takes offence and it's all ruined.

'I'll wake you in a couple of hours, mum.'

She sighs as she walks out. 'Oh, I doubt I'll be able to sleep, love. I'm too churned up to relax.'

Rick pulls up in the lane outside an hour later. I meet him at the front door with a finger pressed to my lips and shut us both into the kitchen where our talking won't disturb mum. He smiles a little when he hears her snoring through the living room door. 'So that's who you've inherited it from.'

He looks tired but composed. No sign of the anguish that's been my lot since last night. I have to resist a cruel desire to say something horrible just to see his face fall and know that he cares. We sit at the table but don't touch.

'I'll leave for the mainland on the last ferry tonight,' he tells me, 'if you want me to.'

I get up to make coffee. I know he's following me with his eyes as I move around the room but I avoid his gaze until I'm sat opposite him again, and then I stretch my fingers across the table and touch them to his. 'Don't go. Don't ever go.' I watch him carefully.

He blinks at me. 'What do you mean?'

We've never come close to this before, to a serious discussion of Our Future, and I know that's been entirely down to me. I chose to believe my sidestepping and my silence were evidence that I had a conscience buried beneath my desire for him. If I never asked about his wife, never let him even suggest the possibility of leaving her, then the damage done could be repairable. But, like mum, I was just selfishly pursuing my own skewed love-ideal, keeping him at arm's length so that I wouldn't have to surrender the fantasy.

'Leave her. Or leave me if you can't leave her. No, leave her. I want you to stay.'

I can't take it back now. I don't think I want to. The relief is tremendous and I know I'm smiling too widely for such a solemn moment but I can't help it. It doesn't last long. Rick stares at me until my mouth is a dry, tight line and my hands are shaking. I hadn't considered his response, hadn't ventured any further in my thought process than overcoming my own lifetime's fears and failings, but now I do. In the moment before he speaks I think I've lost him and I know I can't bear it.

'But how can I trust you, Fern?' he asks. 'What if this is another one of your games and you change your mind tomorrow?'

So it's not an outright rejection. The relief makes me smile again. 'It's not a game, I promise. I want you to be just mine, and I want us to raise our child together. I want you to leave your wife.'

He still doesn't move to touch me and he's not smiling. I try to think of something else to say, something more persuasive, but panic has emptied my mind so I just sit in silence and wait.

'I know I'm supposed to be the villain of the piece, the married man dangling two women's hearts,' he says slowly, looking down at the table and then back at me, 'but with you I feel more like the victim.' He ignores my gasp. 'You lie to me, Fern, you lie all the time, about everything. I don't know who you are; I don't know anything about your life. You've never let me.'

He holds his hand up to stop me from speaking. 'I know you love me, but on your screwed up terms, always on your terms. I think you like this situation we have, you get a kick out of it, and I don't believe you really want to change anything. You don't want intimacy. You don't want me to know you.' He takes a deep breath in. 'So, if you really mean it about me leaving her, you're going to have to prove it to me. Your word just isn't good enough anymore.'

This is it. This is the damage I've done. It's sitting opposite me in the shape of the man I love and telling me I'm not to be trusted. And he's right. Of course he's right. But I don't want that life anymore. I don't want to raise a child and begrudge every moment that child takes from my other love. I don't want to make my child believe their father doesn't love them, and I don't want to blame them when their father eventually leaves. Because he will leave, if I don't change.

Maybe that's why my own father left us. Not because of me, or because he got bored of us, but because my mother denied him any real place in her life. She didn't want him to exist in any concrete sense.

I stand up and walk around the table, put my hands either

side of Rick's face and kiss him on the mouth. 'You're right,' I tell him. 'You're right about all of it. I keep secrets as if my life depended on it, and I deceive people as a matter of course. It's so ingrained an impulse that it doesn't even feel wrong. I don't want to blame mum, but she's the same as me. Or, I'm the same as her. We've always been like that.'

I reach over and take the padded envelope from the dresser drawer, and I lay it on the table in front of him. He looks confused.

'My father left when I was nine,' I say. 'He was married, like you, and my mother loved him more than anything. She loved him more than she loved me. She didn't know anything about him, not even where he lived, but she liked it that way. I've been trying to find out what happened to him, for her and for me. Open the envelope. Tell me what's inside.'

He still looks confused but he tears the seal and pulls out the contents. We both stare down at them.

A letter, in my granny's handwriting. The only letter she ever actually sent to her sister.

And a book. Granny Ivy's *Cooking Book*. Leather-bound, black, cracked across its thick spine. I shiver when I see it.

Rick passes me the letter. I start to read it aloud.

Dear Rose,   April 18th '76
Well, it's been over thirty years since I last saw you. I hope you're done with hating me by now. I hope you're still alive. I need your help.

You always said I was a menace when I had my spell book in front of me, and how right you were. The love charm on the third page, I'm ashamed to admit, is one I made determined use of back when we were young and both in love. I'm sure you always suspected that.

I enclose the book with this letter. I think it's time I put it aside for good and I want you to have it. Please keep it safe. Destroy it if you must, but I'd rather you didn't.

I've been thinking a lot about us over the last months, trying to imagine how different my life could have been with your love, and wondering whether you think of me at all. I've been using you as an empty vessel over the years, a blank wall to store my words. Letter after letter, and none of them sent. But now I've tied a knot that cannot be untied, have perhaps gone too far with my magics, and so I have purchased a postage stamp.

I'm sure you will have received news of me over these last decades, as I have of you. I'm sure you know that Edgar's dead, and that we had a daughter, and now I have a granddaughter. The most beautiful little pumpkin the world ever created. For her if not for me, please help me. I couldn't bear for her to hate me.

I won't spell it out for you, Rose. I flatter myself that we are still bound as sisters in our hearts, and so you will know what I mean when I say that I have put something in the oak tree that stands in our back garden. It's so strong, the oak, and guards us all so well, I'm sure it's the safest place, I just hope I haven't asked too much of it. I'd hate to watch it weaken and rot and know the fault is mine. If I die before you, and I believe that I will, then please come and get what I've hidden and take it far away. Bury it and then forget about it. By then I can't imagine it will matter much what happens to it. For now, I want it close to me, where I can deal with it quickly should I need to change my mind.

Maybe I'm worrying too much? Maybe I'm just a silly old woman with pretensions towards meddling in things that are really no more than hocus pocus? A little excitement to shore up the lonely evenings. I suppose only time will tell.

I'm particularly maudlin tonight. Memories of Edgar haunt

me and the need to feel his warm, living skin beneath my fingertips has me doubled and writhing in my armchair. Who would have thought you could miss a person so much, after so long, that it has the strength to bend your physical form into such shapes of loss?

I'm not going to write any more now but my address is at the top of the page should you ever care to visit or write back to me. I would like that very much.

Love has always been the driving force of my life and this thing I have done, this final spell, though it may look like hate, it is in fact an act of love. I believe that.

Thank you, Rose.

Ivy

I look through the spell book and then push it across the table towards Rick. Tears scuff my vision and I can't make out his expression.

'The last spell,' I say. He starts to read it.

A Ridding Spell

Perform this with humility, for the ripples spreading out from this spell, ripples that you will create by disturbing the natural flow of fate's waters, may reach further and cause more damage than ever you imagined.
Take something of intimacy from the one.

Nail clippings
A lock of hair
A scrap of well used handkerchief
Underthings

Any of these will suffice if imbued
with the one's bodily emanations.

Melt a good-sized piece of black wax until it is
soft and pliant
and shape from this the figure of the one.
Press that which you have taken into the wax
figure and allow to harden.
Paint over with tar. Layer upon layer.
Allow to dry.
Form a pouch from the thickest piece of blackest velvet.
Sew the figure inside it.
Take time to ensure there is no penetration
of light or air.
Secrete the pouch in a place no human eye will uncover.
And then wait.
It will not be long.

To reverse the spell

remove the pouch from its hiding place.
Snip the stitches with a blade of steel.
Release the wax figure and smash it roughly
until it is in a multitude of fragments,
returned to the world from which it was banished.
<u>*You will suffer poor health for some time afterwards*</u>
<u>*or forever afterwards.*</u>

I get up and walk outside. I have to put out a hand to anchor myself when I reach the tree so that I don't trip over its thrusting roots. *I've put something in the oak*. That mossy cleft had been my own hiding place too, a decade ago.

The plastic garden chair sags but holds my weight as I climb onto it. Rick appears beside me, still holding the spell book. He reaches a hand to steady me as I slip an arm inside the tree. I start to pull things out and drop them to the grass at my side. Bundles, soft and hard, wrapped in fabric and oilskin and plastic. I reach and remove until there's nothing left inside the nook and then I get down from the chair.

Mum's at the window now, shouting at me. She disappears and then she's at the door, rushing across the lawn in her slippers, stumbling and swearing and then by my side. She tries to grab me but I ignore her. I don't think she's even seen Rick.

I know what the first object is and I unwrap it from its pillowcase with barely a glance and lay it on the lawn. Mum snatches it up and starts to hurry away with it pressed to her chest but then looks down, falters and turns back.

'This isn't mine. Who are these people?'

The next bundle. A silk bag, half rotted through. It spills a bright shower of gemstones over my feet. Quartz, carnelian and jasper. Amethyst and moonstone. Granny Ivy's cache of crystals. Mum bends and scrabbles to scoop them up then stares and lets them trickle back through her fingers to the ground.

Something hard, stitched inside black velvet. I try to tear the material and manage to create a hole large enough to force part of the object through. A crude wax figure, coated in tar and matted with hair. Mum tries to take it from me but I push her away.

'Don't touch it.'

And finally one of my old exercise books in a plastic bag, covered with Christmas wrapping paper. My name scribbled out. The pages are bulky and brittle, held together with staples and memories. A scrapbook. Photographs of my father have been glued inside. A page from a map book. A silver chain. I look at mum. She stands with her head down and her hand out, waiting.

I lay the book gently across her open palm and bend to gather up the rest of the items as she turns away and walks back inside the house.

Two Photographs Of A Man Asleep

It was late evening. We'd been sleeping, fitted one inside the other like a Japanese puzzle box. Exhaustion made instant statues of us. Your mouth still fastened on my breast. My fingers curled into your hair.

I released myself and turned my head and saw the camera you'd bought me, laying on the bedside cabinet. The noise it made when I pressed the little button was enough to wake you.

Click.

You didn't open your eyes but you reached out a hand and pulled me back to rest beside you. You were smiling. You looked so beautiful.

I tucked the camera beneath my pillow. I kissed your eyelids. And we curled into each other and slept through the night, right through, until checkout.

I wanted just one more. One more, just for me.

I wanted an image that would slip between my ribs and wrap itself around my heart, whenever I became flinty with resentment. Paper defeats rock.

Click.

And then I wanted another one. When you were insecure, you'd get a certain look. Your uncertain look. Think of a child threatened with a slap if they don't do their sums correctly. Try as I might, I could never recall that look from memory.

Click.

It wasn't enough. I wanted more. I deserved more.

I wanted to steal a photograph for every mood, every occasion. Have so many images of you that I could stitch your smile into my pillowcase and sleep cheek to cheek with you at night. Turn you into a brooch and pin you to my blouse like a nametag. Cut you down the middle and jumble you up and recreate you. Make a collage of your body.

I wanted so many photographs that I could waste them, take them by the fistful and step out into a gale and scatter them, and not mind the loss.

Click.

Click.

Click.

There were surely times that you noticed. You must have noticed. But you never stopped me, and you never took the camera away. Why was that?

So I added to my secret haul over the years, stalking the perfect image the way a lepidopterist stalks the rarest butterfly, coveting, catching you in my black and white net, and then pinning you down for evermore.

The last time I saw you, I had my camera with me but it was empty of film. Maybe if I'd had the chance to take your photograph then it would have revealed something about your intentions. I could have studied it afterwards and found something in your expression, a coldness around your mouth, a distance in your eyes, that would have told me you were about to leave me.

Something that would have told me why.

IO

I was twenty-three when I met him. Rick. Three months away from home and my mother. Three lonely months and still hollowed from the medication I'd weaned myself off. Still fighting the mornings.

Mum had prophesised another emotional collapse when I left her. She thrashed around the confines of my room as I packed, threatened to change the locks so that I would never be able to return. She couldn't understand why I'd want to risk breaking myself again on life when she made it so easy for me to stay with her and peep at the world from behind closed curtains. We could wait together for him, for my father, and I could keep her company. As Tommy drove me away from the house I vowed it would be for the final time. I was done with this island. This time I meant it.

I got a job in a cafe and phoned Tommy to give him my new address. I made him promise not to pass it onto mum and I put the phone down on him when he tried to talk to me about her. That still makes me feel guilty, though I'm not sure whether the guilt is more for him or for her. I've always seen them as a pair, I suppose. My screwed up version of family.

So I woke up and went to work and went home and went to bed. And then I woke up and did it all again. When I had free time I walked to tire myself out. If asked, I would have said I was happy enough, until I met him.

The teapot was hot and clasped awkwardly so that it pressed down on the pulse in my wrist. I rushed the last few steps to his table and released it with a hiss of relief, leaning too close, making him swing round. His fingernails, the longest I'd ever seen on a man, scratched a long thin seam across the soft freckles of my elbow.

We both apologised and he tried to take my arm and look at the mark he'd left on me, while I tried to wipe at the spilled water and step away. The cafe was busy and heads swivelled to follow my course, eyes only an hour or two open squinting questions and demands. He stood and dabbed at me with a serviette, helpless in his contrition but determined not to let me go until I'd accepted his offering.

Please, let me see. Use this.

The skin was already raised around the scratch, puffed and putty-white. The trail of red at its centre glistened with moisture but didn't bleed. I thrust my arm out quickly then pulled it back and turned to go.

It was just an accident. It's fine. See.

His watchfulness made me clumsy as I circled the room and cleared the tables. I was relieved when he left.

Later, at home in my flat with the radio on, trying not to hear the resentful whine of next door's daily deserted dachshund, I looked again at my elbow and saw in the shallow trench flecks of deepest blue. They floated below the jelly of the forming scab like glitter in a snow globe and sparked in the lamplight when I moved my arm.

The next time he came into the cafe I was wearing a long-sleeved shirt despite the heat and he didn't see the bandage beneath the cream cotton. My skin smarted with infection, the blue flecks drowning in a tumult of thickened flesh. He asked how I was healing and I pretended not to remember but then couldn't resist asking a question of my own.

Are you an artist?

He laughed and leaned back in his chair, focused entirely on me. I tried not to scratch at my arm.

No, I do the accounts for a building firm. I paint when I can, but not well. Why do you ask?

I shrugged and wiped my hands on my apron front. I couldn't tell him that each beat of my heart, each spurt of blood through my veins, was taking a part of him, of his creativity, deeper into my body. For a moment I considered asking him the name of the exact shade of blue he used in his painting. Azure? Cerulean? Periwinkle? But he was smiling up at me and waiting for me to respond, those long fingernails stroking his cheek lightly, and I knew that if I spoke I'd start to stammer. So I just shrugged again and smiled back at him until my manager called out an order.

He raised a hand in farewell when he left. One of the other waitresses, face impenetrable beneath rainbow blocks of powder, nudged me with a leer.

*You've got yourself an admirer. It's a pity he's married or you'd
have to watch out; I'd have a go on him myself.*

I ignored him the next time he came into the cafe, tidying the
tables around his stare without ever once looking directly at
him. But I saw the ring on his finger and wondered why I
hadn't noticed it before. My arm throbbed poison, leaking pus
into the bandage that bulked out my blouse sleeve. I'd lanced
the cut myself with a pin, pricking channels of release into
the suppuration and examining the muddy discharge for blue.
But what colour would it be now that it was folded into my
body's own mix of hue?

My face was stiff with the effort not to meet his eye, flushed
with heat. When he left, he looked back at me and raised a
hand again but I turned away.

That night I dreamt of my mother. She was drowning in an
artist's palette, floundering between the hollows that
separated the colours, pulling herself free and then slipping
back down. Whenever she opened her mouth to scream, rich,
thick purple paint flowed from her mouth and ran down her
chin. Her chest was marbled with it.

On my day off, I made an appointment with the doctor but
then didn't leave my flat. The tenants above and below me
argued in perfect rhythm, vowels thumping and distorted. The
dachshund howled a chorus and I wore my earplugs while I
soaked the wound and lifted the fierce scab, wiping the
exposed pit with disinfectant and then wrapping it in paper
towels.

By the following week my elbow was too swollen to fit into
the sleeve of my blouse so I wore a loose jumper to work.
When my manager saw me she told me to go home and
change. I stumbled into tables as I walked away and had to

grab at the coat rack by the door to steady myself. For a moment, face pillowed in the damp, cool folds of fabric, I wished I was at home with my mother, but I crushed the thought in my fist and dropped it on the pavement as I hauled myself out onto the street.

He was standing by the kerb as if he'd been waiting there for me. His arms were around me before I could even stretch mine out to him and he held me against his chest as he raised a hand for a taxi.

I remember only fragments of that drive to the hospital but I know I cried as I tried to wriggle out of my jumper to show him the point at which he'd entered my body and claimed a place beneath my skin. I remember he hushed me and pulled my jumper back down while the taxi driver pretended not to watch.

The hospital staff were efficient and unimpressed. They cut and cleaned while I shivered and he held my hand. He didn't contradict them when they assumed he was mine, and he read the little square of instructions on the antibiotics bottle as closely as if he would be by my side through the next week to make sure they were taken correctly. His name in my mouth numbed the tip of my tongue like Novocain.

Dusk had dampened the pavements by the time we emerged. We stood silently together at the hospital entrance to wait for a taxi, his arm around my shoulders. He got out with me when we reached my flat, paid the driver and led the way to the main door.

Inside the murk of the corridor he faltered and I thought he was going to leave then, say something apologetic and hurry back outside, but he was just unsure which floor was mine. I passed him the key and he took my hand as we mounted the stairs.

The flat was chilled from the open windows. He sorted through cupboards while I bathed, heated canned soup and insisted I ate it. I was drowsy and sore, tensed against his eventual departure. I stood up and said something dismissive, something rude, but he laughed and walked ahead of me into the bedroom, turned back the covers on the bed and began to undress. I leant against the doorframe and watched his body rise up from the fallen fabric, sepia skin against the backwash of street lamps. I lay down beside him.

Later, he traced those long nails around my arms, following the vein's twisted path down to my wrists.

Where are they now?

I tapped my chest.

They're in here. If you cut me open you'd find them all speckled inside my heart. A Faberge egg.

After he woke, when the night was starting to break apart at the edges, he said:

It's called Celeste. That shade of blue I use.

*

They're all spread out on the table in front of me. I try to slow my thoughts down before acting, make myself move to switch the kettle on and then spoon coffee into mugs. Rick stands by the door and stares. He doesn't understand much of what's going on but I can tell from the purse of his lips that the little that has sunk in is distasteful. I can't blame him his repulsion.

200

He came to visit me thinking it would be a lovely, loving surprise and now he's stuck in this house with two mad women, the prospect of fatherhood and the legacy of my granny's witchcraft. But this is what it is. This is me.

Memory rustles the hem of a dark skirt across my hand, trails it over my fingers and then flicks it away before I can grab hold. I'm left with the tastes of chocolate and ginger, tear-salted and slightly bitter. I sit and try to empty my mind, let my senses snag it close enough to touch.

And then it's there. *She's* there in the room with me, and I'm four again and crouched at my granny's feet, safe in the stiff drape of her skirts, giving her straggles of my father's hair in exchange for the biscuit tin. Cramming my mouth full as I watch her tie them into a delicate knot and tuck them into a pocket. A magical insurance policy. Just in case they're ever needed. So, mum was right; it really was my fault that my father disappeared. Or at least in part my fault.

I want to rush and tell her, confess my complicity. Where is she anyway? I look past Rick, through the open door. There's nobody in the hallway and when I lean to the side I can see that she's not in her armchair in the living room either. She must surely be in her room, leafing through her scrapbook. Probably furious with me for uncovering her secrets when she'd thought they were so well hidden. Yet another finally exposed to daylight. But I can make this better. I can bring him back. It said so in Granny Ivy's spell book.

I don't pause to allow rationality so much as a raised hand. I stand up and get the scissors from the dresser drawer. Rick moves in front of me to block my return to the table. 'What the hell are you doing?' he asks.

He's got me by the arms and I flail against him as I try to push past. The scissors slice the air in front of his nose and he grips my wrist to force it down. My breath's starting to form lumps in my chest now, sobs like stones trying to rise up and escape through my mouth, rattling against my teeth. 'I have to set it free,' I tell him. 'Do you know what she did? I have to set him free.'

The moment he releases me I'm calm again. He shrugs his helplessness but nods and steps back. I love him so much then, for not telling me to stop being silly, stop being hysterical. Typical pregnant woman, drifting on a wave of hormones into a world of fantasy.

I slide the scissors against the bag and snip at its stitches, one after another. Despite himself, Rick steps forward to watch. As the velvet folds back my fingertips start to numb. There's something repulsive about the wax lump concealed inside and I don't want to touch it. A single hair, thick with tar, bristles into the daylight. Hinged and angular like a spider's leg. Behind me, Rick makes a disgusted noise. Then something shifts deeper inside the pouch and a web of spiders bursts across my imagination, scurrying in their hundreds across the table, up my arms. Even when I throw the tea towel over it I'm sure I can see it move and it's only when I'm in the hallway with the kitchen door slammed shut against it and Rick's arms around me that I can control the urge to scream.

'Shit, Fern,' he whispers, and I can tell how spooked he is. 'Don't touch that thing. Let me just put it in the bin, okay?'

I shake my head. 'It's not my choice to make. It's hers.' I nod my head towards the ceiling. 'If there's a chance...'

His hand is cold against mine as he leads me into the living room and shuts the door behind us. He pushes me gently into mum's armchair and crouches beside me. 'Of course there's no chance. This isn't why your dad disappeared. Your grandmother didn't make it happen with magic. For god's sake, Fern, you need to get a grip. It's awful and of course it's upsetting, but your dad walked out on you and your mum. He wasn't torn from you by an evil witch and her spell book. This isn't a fairy tale.'

I try not to spit some automatic defence of Granny Ivy and her magic. 'Mum needs to know.'

He shakes his head. 'No, she doesn't. How will she cope with hearing that about her own mother? No matter whether she believes it or not, it's going to hurt her. It would be cruel to tell her.'

I think he's right and I hate that. 'But it's my fault,' I whisper to him. 'I gave Granny Ivy his hair when I was little. Without that she wouldn't have been able to do the spell. Mum needs to know that it's my fault.'

He hugs me then. 'It's not your fault, darling. It's not even real. Your dad left you. Just let me get rid of that thing in the kitchen before your mum comes downstairs.'

I get to my feet. I'm sure I can hear it hissing at me through the walls. 'No, I'll do it. I need to do it.'

I shudder as I fold the edges of the tea towel around the misshapen bundle, trying not to touch the thing beneath. For a moment, as it's held out in front of me, its weight dragging my wrists down, I want to drop it on the floor and stamp on it. Rip it free from its bindings and smear it across the tiles and leave it there in the sunlight, just to see what will happen.

But I don't.

When the hole's big enough I let the spade fall to the ground. I look up at mum's bedroom window. It's wide open, swinging loose in the breeze, but the curtains are drawn. Rick's standing on the doorstep, watching me.

I drop it in.

The shape hunched at the bottom of the hole looks small and innocuous, even a bit silly in its colourful teacloth wrapping. But then a trickle of earth nudges down onto it and it twitches with the pressure, as if alive. I cover it over as quickly as I can, slapping the spade down when I've finished, holding my hands out stiff in front of me so that they don't touch any part of my body.

It's done.

Rick steers me into the house, rubbing my back and murmuring nonsense words of love. Then he leaves me for a while. To go for a walk, he says, but I know he needs to think, maybe to phone his wife. He kisses me goodbye and promises to be back before dark. I nod. We'll see.

After I've scrubbed my hands at the sink, scrubbed the table and the floor, I stand in the hallway and listen to the house as it releases its day's warmth and settles into its late afternoon rhythms. Then I try to focus past those immediate, comforting sounds and listen for any sign that mum is awake, alive and in the house.

There's no noise from above me, nothing to reassure me that I'm not alone. When I call out there's no answer. She's left me. She knows what I did and she knows what's buried in the garden. No mother could forgive such a betrayal of love, but especially not my mother. Or she's died. She looked out of the window and saw me with my spade and dad's effigy and the shock killed her.

Every stair tread groans beneath the slow plant of my feet as I make my way upstairs. There's dust gathered between each spindle, striped grey where it's worked its way into the crackles of aged gloss. These hidden away places haven't been cleaned

204

since Granny Ivy was alive. How many years? There might even be some residue of her left in the fractured paintwork. Particles of skin and spite left behind. I'll fill a bowl with hot water and bleach later, and clean it all up. Get rid of any trace of her. But I don't mean that, not really. You can forgive so much as an adult if you loved the person when you were young, and I loved her with all my fierce child's heart.

Mum's bedroom door is closed. She must have heard me mount the stairs, if she's still here, but there's no sound at all. I swallow panic and start to run down the landing. I launch myself into her room. She's lying on the bed, propped by pillows, her scrapbook spread across her lap. Her head hangs low on her neck, bobbing over an open page, and she doesn't look up, doesn't move.

When I clamber onto the bed and start shaking her legs, pulling at her dressing gown, she flinches away and one of her slippers jerks from her foot, into my lap. She levers herself up and cradles the book to her chest, looks blankly at me as I cling onto fistfuls of her gown and bend my head to rest it on her shins.

'I thought you'd left me. I'm so sorry, mum, I didn't mean it.'

She can't see me, for a moment, though her eyes are on me. We've been here before, she and I, and all I can do is wait for her to re-focus, to come back from the past and frame me once more within the boundaries of her world. There were times when I found it irritating but right now I'm terrified. It's all I can do not to raise a hand to my mouth and bite, to check that I'm actually here and I do exist.

Then her eyelids flicker and I can see myself duplicated in her irises, outlined in miniature. I feel such relief. She shifts slightly to free herself from my weight and a smile perches high on her cheekbones. Her hand strokes the many robins and snowmen splashed over the book cover, sweeping in gentle circles as if she's stroking the skin of a loved one and is enraptured by the feel of their flesh against hers.

'I'd forgotten. Fern, I'd forgotten it. But it's like he's here with me again, right now.'

She raises the scrapbook and turns a couple of pages then holds it out to me, just quickly, before angling it jealously away. The silver chain dangles from its safety pin, severing the words she's written. I remember that day, going fishing with them both. I remember the flash of light in my net.

She turns another page. A dried fern leaf. I lean closer to read what she's written about me but she pulls back, out of reach, and turns the pages until they're blank. Then she closes the book and opens it again, starting at the beginning. Her lips twitch as she reads. I sit beside her and wait until she's finished. She's still smiling when she slides a finger between the first pages ready to return to the start once more. I can see a scrap of dark fabric but she lays the book across her chest then and resumes the rhythmic stroking. She can't bear to not be touching it.

'I'd forgotten the feeling of how it felt, being with him. Loving him. Not even a photograph managed to bring that fully to life. But this...' She bends her head and sniffs at one of the snowmen. 'This is us. This is him. My memories. When I read these, Fern, I can actually smell him. He's so here I can actually see the dent his body's making on the mattress as he sits beside me.'

I find myself looking at the area she's waving her hand over, straining to see what she's seeing. 'But if it means that much to you, why did you leave it in the oak? You could have got it out at anytime.'

She laughs and clutches the book closer to her throat. 'Because I got scared. I waited for so long and then I believed he'd never come back while I contented myself with this pale copy of what we had. I couldn't bear to destroy it so I dropped it into the tree. But you freed him for me, you gave him back to me, and he hasn't changed a bit, Fern. He's still him.'

I'm dying to take the book from her and read it through for myself but there's no way she'd let me. It's hers and just hers. The way my father was hers and just hers. She'll never share him.

I can smile, though, at her joy. 'But he has to have changed, mum, over the years.'

She shakes her head and brings her fist up to her temple. 'Not in here he hasn't. He's just the same.'

There's nothing more to say. Before I leave the room she's opened the scrapbook again and I don't think she even knows I've gone. When I look back her face has loosened into a gasp as the words she's written unravel across her memory. I'll never know what's in there, but I can guess and if I want to I can make it up. Imagine their love affair and recreate it for myself. The first glimpse through to the last kiss, and every scene between. That way I'll have a piece of him too.

Tommy taps on the window when I'm peeling potatoes for dinner and I shriek and nearly chop the end of my thumb off. I'd been listening out for a car in the lane but he must have walked the couple of miles to get here. I wave him round to the door but he stays where he is and waves back. *Come out here.*

'You scared me.' I hug him and peer over his shoulder to the gate. It's nearly entirely night now.

'I'm sorry, love, but I wanted to talk to you alone. Where's your young man?'

I shrug. 'He just popped out. He'll be back soon, and mum's upstairs.'

'I haven't spotted you at the viewing point for the last couple of days.' Tommy smiles at me. 'I was hoping I'd see you.'

'Oh, I've stopped driving up there now. Once you've seen a few ferries going in and out you've seen them all.' I laugh and shiver. 'Won't you come in? I'm making dinner. Mum should be down soon, it's way past gin o'clock.'

He narrows his eyes at me. 'You really don't want to know what I've got to say, do you? So you've read the letter your granny sent her sister?'

I nod and focus on his face. No more avoidance. 'Yes. And you knew. She told you what she was going to do, didn't she?'

Tommy draws his breath in sharply and looks at the ground. 'You must hate me. I'm sorry, love. I won't make excuses. Just believe I'm sorry. But your mum, does she know?'

He rubs at his arms and hunches into himself as he waits for the answer. Such fear for her, and such love. How could I hate him?

'No, she doesn't know. She doesn't need to.' I watch him sag with relief and when he raises his head the corrugations around his eyes have smoothed out. He grasps at me.

'Oh, that's a weight off, love. The last thing I'd have wanted was to hurt her. You know she didn't want me involved, your granny. She didn't tell me much but I knew she was planning something, something magical, to get rid of him. I didn't pay much mind but then your dad just stopped coming round so I asked her about it. I felt a bit silly if I'm honest, but she told me she'd done a spell and her sister would take care of things if it were needed.' He's babbling now. 'And then you said you were going to visit her and I started worrying that she'd let something slip or just outright tell you. And the thought of your mum finding something like that out, and of knowing that I'd known, well, it didn't bear thinking about.'

I take the hand that's squeezing my arm and hold it for a moment. 'I don't want to hear any more. In order to keep on loving Granny Ivy and you, I need to not know any more of what she did. Okay? Now, come inside and have a drink. Please.'

He allows himself to be led around the house and into the warmth of the kitchen. I call to mum and she shouts an answer. I can hear her banging around up in her room. No doubt hunting down another hiding place for her scrapbook. Maybe I should give her a list of all the places not to hide it if she doesn't want it to be found.

'What are you going to do now?' Tommy asks me as he puts the kettle on. 'About finding out what happened to him? You don't really believe all that about your granny making him disappear, do you?'

I return to the sink and the potatoes. From here I can keep an eye on the lane. 'I don't know what I'm going to do. Probably nothing. I don't think mum really wants to know, not deep down, and maybe it's better that I don't. He left us. I should leave it at that.'

The trees that line the lane are suddenly bleached and bright, bony against the black sky. I tense as I wait to see if this car will stop. Behind me, Tommy fidgets with his glass.

'But surely you want to know? What if he's still alive?'

A car glides to a halt just past the gate. He's back.

I look at Tommy. 'He left us. He went back to his wife. That's it. There's nothing else to find out.' I walk out into the hall so that I can meet Rick at the door.

There are streaks of dried tears across his cheekbones but he smiles when he sees me, and nods. His travel bag is slung over his shoulder. As I watch him walk up the stairs to put it in my room and hear him speak to mum as he passes her on the landing, I stand in the gloom of the hallway and finally let myself think of her. The wife. The wronged woman. I gave him a choice, one that my mother never gave my father, and he chose me. I want to meet her and tell her I'm sorry but I know that'll never happen. You don't get to be sorry in situations like these.

Mum grins at me when she comes downstairs, mouth wide and greasy and maroon. I'm sure that's the same lipstick she's had since I was a girl and it hasn't aged well. I think about pointing that out, maybe giving her a tissue for the excess that has clumped between her front teeth, but she winks and points at the ceiling, slaps at my arm as if I've achieved something clever, and I just smile back and nod. There's something grotesque about her delight and I hope she can wipe the grin off before Rick comes back down.

In the brighter light of the kitchen I see that she's wearing the silver chain I caught in my net so many years ago. Its tarnish has stained her throat brown. I try not to stare. She really doesn't want me to look for my dad, then. If she did, or if she believed there was a chance he'd come back, she wouldn't even think of publicising this example of her deceit. The irony of the situation makes me bitter suddenly. All these years, not thinking about him, never wanting to see him again, and now I do want it, so much, and it's too late. Mum's content with her memories. He'll never age for her now, and he'll never stop loving her.

Tommy finishes his drink and refuses another. He kisses mum gently on the forehead and I walk with him to the front door.

'He did love you, your dad,' he says to me. 'The times I saw him with you, he was lit up with it. I followed him back to the dock once, when you were only a toddler, and I gave him a shove or two. Threatened him with all sorts if he came back. I still hoped, then, that Iris might give me a chance, especially with a baby to think about. He was scared, I could tell, but he was back a couple of weeks later. I never spoke to him after that. There was nothing more to say. I don't know why he left in the end, or where he went, but it won't have been because he didn't love either of you enough.'

His kindness makes me long to press my cheek into his chest and cry for a while. He doesn't understand that if I want to believe dad wouldn't have left us willingly, then I have to believe Granny Ivy's magic disposed of him in some awful way, and I don't want to believe that. I don't ever want to think of that again. But there is another option; that he loved us all and he would have carried on with his complicated juggling of wife, lover and child for as long as he could, only something happened to him. A heart attack, or a car accident. Something that wasn't the result of a lack of love or my granny's malevolence. If I choose to look for him then I'll have to be prepared to find that out, and then live with it. I'm not sure that I am prepared. He loved us. He left us. Maybe that can be enough.

When I go back in Rick's pouring mum a gin and looking strained. I kiss him and sit down at the table. Mum's grinning like a circus clown, lipstick smeared all around her mouth. I frown at her and wiggle a finger over my own face but she doesn't seem to understand.

'Champagne,' she announces. 'There's a bottle in the cupboard. I was saving it for something else but I think we should open it tonight. We've got something to celebrate.'

Both Rick and I wince. I try to catch his eye, to mouth an apology, but he keeps his back turned as he cuts a lemon into slices. I kick out at mum under the table and shake my head but she stands up bossily and points at the broom cupboard in the corner of the room. 'It's in there, Rick, could you get it out please? It's on the floor behind the bread-maker.' She shoots me a triumphant glance. She's better at hiding things than I gave her credit for.

As Rick eases the cork out of the bottle with a pained look, I know I have to rescue him from this before mum's lack of tact sends him running for his car. 'So, mum, you and Tommy,' I say, leaning towards her with my chin propped on my palms. 'Was it a regular thing or just the once?'

She reddens immediately and the lipstick disappears against the backdrop of her skin. 'I don't know what you're talking about.'

'Of course you do,' I tell her. 'The other night, when Tommy was here, you both let it slip that you'd enjoyed some... intimacy. Something more than friendship. I was just wondering whether it was a regular thing. All those years, when I was away and you had the house to yourself.' I raise my eyebrows at her suggestively. 'Because if you want me and Rick to go out tonight and give you some space...?'

I let the rest of the sentence hang in the air between us and watch it thud down onto the table. Mum, puce now and outraged, stands up. 'What a disgusting thing to say. There was never. It was only the once and it was his fault for bringing the wine over. If you're going to keep going on about it then I'll eat my dinner in the living room.' She turns and rushes out.

I stand up and take the bottle of champagne from Rick. 'It's okay, you don't need to open it.' I put my arms around him and hug him to me. Our sinful love.

'If our daughter falls in love with a married man then I'll kill her,' I say. 'It stops here. With me.' I nuzzle his neck and we sway together for a moment until mum calls out for her gin.

A Page From A Calendar (showing two months)

Nine weeks and three days. The longest you'd ever been away from me. Nine weeks and three days. When I heard your car in the lane I didn't even get up from my bed. It couldn't be you; you couldn't be back. In my imagination you'd died over and over. Burnt to ashes in a house fire. Broken apart in the wreckage of your car. Slithered overboard on the ferry. I knew exactly what your face looked like as you slipped silently into the sea with out-flung arms.

Or you'd woken one morning and pressed your fingers into the velvet pouch of your wife's armpit, pressed them against your face, breathed her in and remembered that you loved her. Remembered just how much.

Or you'd been walking in a grey street, in a grey city, and a finger of late afternoon sun nudged the skin of a beautiful girl, turned her hair to flames, and you gasped and followed her until she turned and noticed you, smiled and took you by the hand.

So it couldn't be you.

Your car horn. My mother's voice raised in sharp exclamation. My daughter's shouts of fury. Pebbles through the open window, earth on the bedroom floor. The oak quivered as I raised myself onto an elbow and upright. Then your face, floating ghostlike through its leaves. My Green Man. Straddled around a branch, too high and reaching for me, laughing. I ran then, and met you in the tangle of roots beneath its canopy, do you remember? Your trousers ruined and your hands scuffed. Twigs your untidy crown.

I didn't care that my mother and my daughter were standing at the door, or that my daughter was crying. The hairs on my body thrust themselves upwards to greet the cup of your palm, electric shock shivers where skin met skin.

You tried to speak and I shook my head. It didn't matter where you'd been. It didn't matter what you'd been doing, or with whom. I blew a kiss to my daughter, nodded at my mother. She nodded back and grasped our child by the wrist, turned away. I held your hand and led you through the garden gate, barefoot and bag-less.

As you drove us down the lane I looked over my shoulder at my open bedroom window and I suddenly wanted, so much, to stop you. I wanted to walk slowly back inside and lie on my bed and feel again the desolation of losing you, but with *this* knowledge gilding its edges. I wanted to hide my face in the pillow, recreate the anguish, hold it in my cheek and suck at it, so that I could have this moment again, now that I knew this moment would come. I almost did stop you, make you turn around, but then you stroked a hand across my thighs and grinned at me and I gasped and folded myself around your warm fingers, and all thought flew from me with my bitten breath.

The next time you stayed away for nine weeks and three days, four days, five days, I lay in my bedroom and imagined you floating faceless through shoals of fish, tattered limbs trailing at your sides, but I kept my brush and lipstick in my pocket, ready.

Acknowledgements

Without the support and encouragement of friends, I would never have had the courage to believe I could finish this novel and send it out into the world. Thank you Rachel Davies for being there from the start, and for your steadfast faith in me, through chapter after chapter. Thank you Gillian Eaton for the wise and sensitive advice and constant enthusiasm. Thank you Charlotte Penny, dear friend and partner in cake-eating crime, for telling me you loved it and for insisting I send it to Parthian.

I was lucky enough to receive guidance from the wonderful poet Samantha Wynne-Rhydderch, and will always be grateful that she never let me off the hook when it came to chasing an image. Thank you Samantha.

Cathy Stocker, I couldn't have wished for a more perfect cover for the novel.

Thanks to my parents for the support they've always shown, and to Simon for the love.

Huge gratitude goes to Richard Davies and the Parthian team. Susie Wild, you are a star of an editor. Thanks for taking a chance on me.

And lastly, thanks to all those writers who have inspired and moved me: my fellow Bards and beyond them, across a world of words.

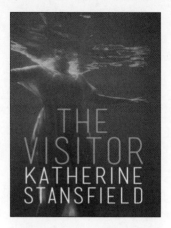

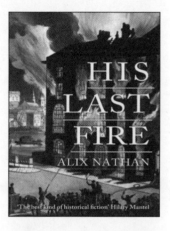

PARTHIAN

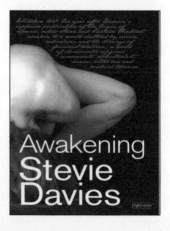